R.I.P.
FIVE STORIES
OF THE
SUPERNATURAL

MORE WILDSIDE CLASSICS

Please see www.wildsidepress.com for a complete list!

R.I.P.
FIVE STORIES
OF THE SUPERNATURAL

Edited by

R. Reginald
and
Douglas Melville

WILDSIDE PRESS

For Doris Illes, without whom ...

R.I.P.
FIVE STORIES
OF THE SUPERNATURAL

This edition published in 2006 by Wildside Press, LLC.
www.wildsidepress.com

CONTENTS

SOULS ON FIFTH

SOULS ON FIFTH
BY GRANVILLE BARKER
WITH FRONTISPIECE
BY NORMAN WILKINSON

BOSTON

LITTLE, BROWN, AND COMPANY

1917

Norwood Press

Set up and electrotyped by J. S. Cushing Co., Norwood, Mass., U.S.A.

Presswork by S. J. Parkhill & Co., Boston, Mass., U.S.A.

SOULS ON FIFTH

SOULS ON FIFTH

MANY times have I paced the relentless street;
on its stones that are harder than stone was ever
meant to be and smoother than any false welcome in the world.

I have paced it at all hours and seasons; when
it was shadowless in a burning sun; with the
snow clouding and whitening the night. Why
I started up it that early autumn morning is
no matter to anyone but myself. But never
had I seen the Avenue emptier, found it more
silent. Day would not dawn yet for an hour.
The sky was clear; as I went it grew opaque,
pressing down upon the world. There was
an eddying wind, which surprised one at the
street corners. Since I was alone and rather
lonelier than that, my spirit sought refuge

Souls on Fifth

among impossible things. Even Fifth Avenue itself was not at that moment very real to me; a place for the body to tire in, that was all.

I had noticed somewhere about Forty-fourth Street, at a good height from the ground, a whirl in the air of what seemed — snow — ashes — dead leaves? Not snow, I thought, and too grey for snow besides. Not ashes; and what should dead leaves do there? I did not stop. By the cathedral there was something curious too. It seemed as if large grey flakes of many shapes and sizes were being blown about and caught upon the crockets of the spires. My eyes are queer tonight, I said. Up against the great door there seemed to be a shadowy drift of grey, thick and fermenting. Still I did not cross the road. I looked about though now for these strange things, and, heavens! when I looked the air of the Avenue was full of them. They were much larger than snowflakes and some were of the queerest shape. One saw them best when they blew up against the sky; though by peering carefully, I could find them too, grey against the grey walls, well above my head. From every corner and crevice the gusty wind was dislodging them, and it seemed as if they clung to the walls. I looked on the ground. I thought I saw several blowing past. I thought I saw one flat and still. I went up to put my foot on it. No, that was only a little facet of the pavement that had lost the reflection of the street lights. Then I turned to go back to inspect the cathedral door.

As I turned, there, quite distinctly, in the corner of a window-sill within my reach was one small grey shape. Against the red stone one couldn't miss it. I went closer. It was thicker than I'd fancied and might have been almost transparent but that it was covered, patchily, with a sort of silvery fur, not unlike the growth on an Edelweiss flower. Beneath the fur it was of a rather mottled dirty grey. There were odd markings on it which might have been made by hand. It was just about as wide at its widest as my palm and as long as a glove would be. But the shape of the shape was no shape you could name, it looked a rag. It was

[5]

indeed very ugly, more like than anything to a dirty little bit of used grey flannel. I noticed that the thing seemed somehow to palpitate. That was queerest of all, though then I remembered the fermenting mass against St. Patrick's door. After a moment I took it gingerly in my hand. It had no weight. But by this time I was so surprised that I think I spoke aloud. "What on earth is it?" I said.

And there seemed to come from it a sound like the echo of a scraped violin, shaping into words which were:

"I am the soul of the late Mrs. Henry Brett van Goylen and I'll trouble you to put me down."

Politely and in some alarm I put her down and as I did so one of the eddying gusts of wind blew the shape of her away.

Thus then I began my search for souls. I caught no more that night for the dawn came soon. But many a night after for an hour or two before the morning broke would I adventure up the Avenue and make my bag. They

Souls on Fifth

were easy to find when you knew how to look, and after a time easy enough to catch. I thought first of buying a butterfly net for the sport but policemen would have noticed that. As it was I had to mind not to loiter long.

I was alone in New York and knew no one, though ten years before, visiting it with my father, a man of some fame, I had known every one there was to know. But now I had only work to do which took me day by day to the library at Forty-second Street. "This time then," I had said, "I will know nobody." It needed not any effort. But now, it seemed, I was to know New Yorkers as they had never been known before.

For a long time it was absorbingly interesting. There were nights on which one couldn't catch a soul. It depended a good deal on the weather, but I soon found out the quite impossible times. When the night was still, they hung — a cubic layer of them, four miles long and more and very thick — a hundred feet or so high in the air. It was some while before I could discover the general laws of their being,

[7]

Souls on Fifth

but I gathered for one thing that, normally, a sort of double river of souls was always flowing up and down Fifth Avenue; not side by side as the traffic flows, but above and below; below, of course, to come up and above to go down. This was the general law; and, in spite of interruptions and scatterings, the flow never ceased. They are supposed to be quite invisible and in nothing like daylight have I ever caught a glimpse of one. Heavy rain is hard on them. It beats them to the ground in a sort of jellified mass. I went out one pouring night to discover what did happen then. For a long time I could see nothing, the wet had made them transparent to my eyes. But soon I found that I was actually treading inches deep in a mess of souls. While such a thing can give them no actual pain yet the indignity of it was great and I felt I could not stop and talk to any of them that night. Besides they were all mashed up one with the other, like jujubes that a child has warmed in its pocket. I should have had to pick them apart.

A blizzard upsets them badly. I remember

Souls on Fifth

a soul telling me that once for a long time she was blown and blown between Forty-second and Forty-fifth Streets, never further either way. She'd get into the stream flowing down, but every time at Forty-second Street, a gust would whirl her up and round, and at Forty-fifth the same thing happened if she'd got into the stream flowing up. She said it went on like that for a year. She probably didn't mean to be inaccurate, (these disembodied beings quickly lose our sense of time) but I've no doubt she was blown about so for some days. It is the light eddying wind which brings them down to earth or near it and scatters them into corners singly or by twos and threes. That was the great weather for soul-hunting and I did my best never to miss a night of it.

From first to last I suppose I had talks with quite five hundred souls. But they were difficult to get on with; that's the truth. I had thought at first that any of them would be thankful for a terrestrial chat. Not a bit of it. In the first place they took no interest whatever in the affairs of the world. They knew of nothing that had happened in it since their deaths and, as a rule, they cared to know nothing. I believe that not more than a dozen times was I questioned. A woman might ask me if I knew her widower, but it was purely to make conversation, the habit of small talk not having died with her. Three men at various times wanted to hear about the last Presidential Election. But two of them I found did not in the least know how long they had been dead; it was Bryan's chances against McKinley they were fussed about. No doubt they had been keen politicians for when they learned that eighteen years had passed since then in which many most serious things had happened to the world, they at once lost all interest.

Usually they would only talk about themselves. They wouldn't even recognize the existence of other souls. They were not more egotistic than they had been in the material world, but now there was no false shame about it, and it was carried to extremes for which even forty years' growing contempt for the human race found me unprepared.

Souls on Fifth

I remember for instance how the lady who was blown wildly for what seemed to her (poor dear!) a year between Forty-fifth and Forty-second Streets, would keep on insisting that such a thing had never happened to any soul before. I sympathized with her for the uncomfortable time she had had; but no, that wasn't enough. She kept at it till I bettered her by saying that, quite obviously, such a thing never could happen to any soul again. Then she was satisfied.

There were exceptions. There was the Reverend Evan Thomas. It was from him indeed that I gathered most information; by his help that I was able to grasp at last what really was happening to them all in this future life.

I found the soul of this once popular preacher on a September night wedged in the shutters of a candy shop. I dug him out and he thanked me. He was about seven inches long by three broad, quite straight down one side, but with undular indentations upon the other; of no thickness to speak of, with rather a rub-

Souls on Fifth

bery surface and in colour a sort of blueish grey. It was a fine night. The harsh gust of wind that had wedged him in the shutter had died down and we had a long and pleasant chat.

He spoke with equal ease and cheerfulness about his past life and his present death. Was this state of things the Heaven he had spent so much time and energy preaching about? No, on the whole he didn't think it was. But in that case had his soul (I had to put this delicately) and the thousands upon thousands of other souls besides that we knew were drifting up and down — had they taken, so to speak, the wrong turning? No, he didn't exactly think that either. I must remember, of course, that he had not been dead long. I must also remember that for many years now the world, or, at any rate, that part of it that lived and moved on Fifth Avenue, had taken Heaven so much for granted that it had become the vaguest of ideas to them and had entirely ceased to believe in Hell. Now people cannot possibly go to places they don't understand or believe in; that stands to reason. And he quoted me a line from the

Souls on Fifth

Acts about the man who died and went to his own place. That had furnished him, he thought, with a solution of this question.

"When I first died," he told me, "and found myself floating lightly about here, I will own that I was puzzled and even — though I had and still have every faith in God's goodness — even a little disappointed. It was true that in the exercise of my calling I had refrained from painting any very definite picture of the state of bliss to which the souls of the righteous should be called. My own congregation was certainly not such a one as I could indulge in any highly coloured or romantic vision of that Future. They were well educated, practical people. Besides, as far as I could see, the use that they did already make of their imagination was very questionable. To say that they used it merely as a stimulus to erotic frivolities would perhaps have been too harsh, though I have at times been tempted to put my complaint in so many words. But what they needed from me surely, was sobering, commonplace morality. Still, let me confess that when it actually came to entering upon a more blessed existence, I had in my secret heart looked forward to something in the nature of a pleasant little surprise. And to find myself drifting —"

"Still drifting," I said, rather wickedly.

He was not to be checked by any mere witticism — "Drifting," he went on, "and for all I know drifting for an eternity up and down Fifth Avenue! — it was disappointing.

"But I reflected. As a rational Christian I was eager to assure myself of God's laws and then to square them, if possible, with the exigencies of any world in which it might please Him to place me. And I have always been ready, nay, anxious to search out my own faults and if necessary to repent of them. So in the course of much drifting and some whirling, often round the very steeple that pointed to heaven from above the pulpit of my late labours, I disinterestedly reviewed my former existence and gathered it up, so to say, as even the longest life may be gathered, into a dozen sentences. See, now, if they do not give you the key to this mystery.

Souls on Fifth

"I remembered my call from a sphere of popular eloquence in England to the church that — well, it can hardly be said to ornament Fifth Avenue, but it is a pleasant comfortable church. I knew nothing of America at that time. But I had heard stories of the luxury of New York women and of financial corruption among the men, and when the flattering offer came I naturally asked myself whether God had not summoned me to scarify, though lovingly, these highly placed sinners, to bring them to repentance and a more humble following in the footsteps of their Lord. I settled, if possible, to turn a surplus of the enormous stipend they were to give me into a trust fund for some sensible and suitable charity —"

I looked. We were opposite the very church.

"Is the stipend so big?" I asked and nodded across.

"When it came to the point," he said, "I found it not big enough. I had a grown-up son and daughters. They had, of course, to mix on terms of equality with my congregation. We had to keep up appearances; the lay patrons of the church expected it. Still we were never seriously in debt.

"To continue —"

"Please," I begged him. I was enjoying it. He had evidently been a preacher of some style.

"My congregation at once impressed me as being made up of charming people, kindly, clever and hospitable, boundlessly hospitable. We spent several weeks, my wife and I, or my eldest daughter and I, night after night, dining with the chief families among them. One should always accept such invitations, one should view the home-life of one's flock. And while I was sampling them, sizing them up, determining by personal and unprejudiced observation upon which most prevalent vice or failing the sword of my spiritual condemnation should first fall, I merely preached week by week, not to be rash, not to be unfair, sermons upon less disputable subjects, sermons that purposely avoided any vital thrusts into that body politic to which I was now the chosen minister.

Souls on Fifth

"They were admirable to preach to; quick to seize on a point, ever ready for those little sub-humorous sallies which are the salt of a sermon, the delight of a preacher who can discreetly indulge in them. One could not hold their attention long, it is true, but it was keen while it lasted. They liked to have their intelligence appealed to, they welcomed my references to the very latest things in science and literature. I projected a series of sermons, in which I proposed to take Sunday by Sunday the works of some famous sceptical philosopher and endeavour to reconcile them with the Christian Ethic. Such a course would not have been possible in England, where, I will confess, the indifference of congregations to my very extensive modern reading and the quotations I could make from it had often nettled me exceedingly. But these New Yorkers, I did find, to use a vulgar phrase, to be both mentally and spiritually a thoroughly up-to-date crowd.

"Not, mind you, that I had weakened in my resolve to scarify them, when need were

and opportunity came, for their deeper sins.
But I had found that they were not children,
they were not fools, that the thing needed
doing well, and from the point of view of a
thorough understanding of the very peculiar
circumstances under which fashionable life
must be lived here, otherwise it had better be
left alone altogether. That thorough understanding I set myself conscientiously to acquire.

"But, dear me!" he broke off. "My twelve
sentences have been much exceeded. Old
habits! And about myself — it is inexcus-
able." Again I begged him to continue.
Quite cheerfully he did.

"I found many difficulties in my way.
Society women undoubtedly did indulge in
outrageous luxury, but the worst offenders
did not come to my church, and to berate them
in their absence would merely have given undeserved satisfaction to the women who did
come and were themselves by no means innocent in the matter. That is a danger in preaching. Your congregation will always imagine that
you are — as one says — getting at their neigh-

bours and not at them. I did make a most strenuous effort, though, to tackle the question of financial corruption. I worked at it for weeks. But it was a very difficult subject, involving a great complication of figures (at which indeed I was never good) as well as several tricky points of difference between State and Federal law which it really needed an expert to solve. But I could not, above all things, risk exposing my ignorance. That would have done more harm than good. The habit that newspapers in this country have of reporting sermons flatters, it is true, but also intimidates. In the end, to my lasting regret, I felt compelled to abandon the idea.

"I remember I made one attempt to deal with the simple sin of over-eating, of which quite 70 per cent. of my congregation were without doubt guilty. I hung the constructive part of the sermon upon the subject of Food Reform, a very popular one just then. But the destructive part had to be too delicately done to make a real effect. It had to be. For had I not myself fed and fed well at most of their tables? And in the flesh I was a little inclined to stoutness.

"And so after a while I found that I slipped into preaching to my congregation only such sermons as my congregation wanted to hear. What else was to be done? They would not otherwise have come to hear me at all, for there is no law to make them, and nowadays precious little public opinion. I should have lost any chance at all of doing good. As it was, by contriving at any cost to be interesting, my church was kept full, and, starting ostensibly from strange and far-away subjects, Wars with the heathen, Greek Legends, or the latest good novel, I never failed I think in the end to bring my hearers, though at the time they might hardly be conscious of it, one small step nearer to Jesus. It is true that a really strong man in my place might have done better before they turned him out. All I can say is that I did the best that was in me. But looking back I see quite clearly now what happened. I had set out to convert Fifth Avenue; it was Fifth Avenue converted me.

Souls on Fifth

"And that, my dear sir, is why, though disembodied, I am still here and why we are all here; poor souls. In our lifetime, this, at its best, was all we strove towards, and in our death we have come 'to our own place.'"

He ceased. His shape had all the time been lying comfortably along my left forearm. I looked up from it to where, in the air above me, the river of souls flowed ceaselessly on. It was a still night now. I could never make out why, since they had absolutely no personal power of volition, some always got along faster than others. On an average they seemed to make about three miles an hour. It was a wonderfully weary sight.

"Who are they, generally speaking?"

"Well," said the preacher's soul, "it's a most curious mixture. There are the tip-top people who used to belong here and never thought there was any further to get. And then there are all the people who badly wanted to get here in their lifetimes and never could."

"I take it that the two sorts don't mix well," I said.

Souls on Fifth

"There again," he went on, "it doesn't work out as you'd expect. We're all here now because we belong here and we know it. There's no escape; and, as we can't control our movements, we've no power now of associating with one lot of souls more than with another. The wind bloweth us where it listeth. So the consequence is that we don't worry much about our behaviour : and the people who are rude by nature are just rude to everybody, and the snobs are snobbish and the cads caddish and the bullies bully and the gentle folk are gentle without any respect of persons. Nothing else is expected of us. It makes a simple world of it."

"Is there no escape, do you say?" I asked him.

"I don't see how there can be," he said rather plaintively. "In the last world you could — what is called — 'make something' of yourself. You could choose your profession and your friends, you could do right or wrong. You could deny your Lord or act up to your faith."

"Could you always?" I argued. "Circumstances handicap one shockingly. We mean to do better than we ever can."

"My friend," said he, "your faith is the thing you do act up to. That's what we have discovered here. God makes no excuses. The pious opinions you hold have no more effect on the soul than a knowledge of the multiplication table."

"But don't you desire to escape now? How about the effect of that?" I pressed him.

For a little he did not answer; I waited patiently. I have forgotten to remark how soon I had found that for talking to a soul the human voice is a clumsy and unnecessary instrument. One could imagine (I did at first) that the shapes emitted queer little sounds, but I cannot see how that actually could be. I believe that one only instinctively clothed the impressions they conveyed direct to one's mind in the tones of a human voice. And with a very little practice one did not need to do that at all. One could communicate with extraordinary swiftness and ease by imagination alone, talk soul to soul, as it were. It is a simple trick, can be practised between human beings while on earth and is indeed the best form of conversation.

After the moment of silence the soul of the reverend gentleman sighed.

"No," he said, "I cannot honestly say that I want to escape for I cannot muster up a belief that there is anything much else to escape to. All the effort I was capable of in that direction I made in my former life. And I am useful here. I really think I am. Our Lord, you will remember, ministered to the spirits in prison. Whenever I am blown against another soul, whenever the wind gathers two or three of us together, I take up the tale of salvation as I used to do on earth. Those, if I chance to hit upon them, who were accustomed to hear me in that church opposite, are a little bored by it perhaps, for naturally I have nothing new to say. But to the others, to those who had to content themselves on their earthly pilgrimage with nothing but the ideal of Fifth Avenue, and with more commonplace spiritual ministrations — to them, I do think that the

Souls on Fifth

Word of Truth as I am inspired to speak it is a comfort. Though of course it cannot now get them on any further, yet if it consoles them in their present station — well, that is one of the main functions of religion, is it not?"

"But to endure this sort of thing through an eternity!" I said.

"My dear young man," he patronized me, "Time is an illusion. I remember so well making this point in one of my most characteristic discourses. Time is what we think it, a minute of agony is an age, a year of happiness is a minute. Doesn't it strike you that an Eternity of boredom may perhaps have no extreme meaning to those who, after all, have spent most of their time in being bored? You cannot measure emptiness. And Eternity is only the emptiness of Time.

"Hadn't you better let me fly now," he added, "and go home? It will be daylight soon and from what you tell me you haven't been to bed for nights."

I took his soul between my finger and thumb.

"I am exceedingly grateful to you," I said.

[25]

Souls on Fifth

"You have thrown light on what was puzzling me much. Do you think we shall meet again?"

"Only by pure chance," he answered. "Unless — I have a fancy, which I have not yet been able to prove, that if there is a true affinity between souls they will come together in God's good time. I had an acquaintance on earth, an interesting fellow, who built up quite an elaborate theory of soul-affinities. But he ended by walking off with a married woman, which was, to say the least, a most immoral anticipation of God's purposes. Since I entered this state, I must own that I have not yet — and it is strange — blown up against my dear wife, who predeceased me by some few years; also that I have only met two of my very intimate friends. My wife was, I am sure, near as well as dear to me on earth, but then Fifth Avenue may not have been very dear to her. Possibly her soul is somewhere at home in England. On the other hand, time and time again I find myself mixed up with souls here that are not at all the sort I should have chosen to associate with before. That puzzles

Souls on Fifth

me. I shall be interested to see if we two do run across each other much. Good night."

I flung him gently into the air. He sailed quickly out of my sight, for the flowing river was dim now almost to extinction. I doubted somehow if we should meet again.

This had been illuminating. I saw at once where by sheer tactlessness I had failed in talking to the souls. I had assumed that they were unhappy. Not a bit of it. They had got what they wanted. Getting that one always speaks of as a state of heaven upon earth. If then, the final and eternal Heaven turns out merely to be a little more of what we want, what sensible man should turn his back on it for that?

Nor could the souls run, of course, to great variety of disposition. Roughly, as the parson said, one could divide them into two classes, the aboriginal population and the invaders. The invaders should have been the more interesting to talk to for they had achieved here what they could only long for in life, and, one might think, were therefore actively enjoying themselves.

Souls on Fifth

But their complaint was that being in an enormous majority they were mostly only blowing up against each other all the time so that they hardly got into touch with the true Fifth Avenue at all. It was of course a great satisfaction to them to find they were really there at last, but they could tell me nothing much about it. And about the places they had lived in on earth they simply would not speak of them at all. Still much could be guessed at by that.

The old inhabitants, the aborigines, were, one gathered, mostly women and butlers; and the butlers who had been sent away to die, were always glad to be back in their element. I looked almost in vain for souls of the mighty men who had built the great houses and lent them their fame. I believe they are mostly to be found down at Wall Street where they and the bankrupts and gamblers must make a busy crowd. I was indeed assured of this by a very ladylike soul. Business, she said, had been the one thing lovely and pleasant to her husband in his life, and in his death she most sincerely trusted he was not divided from it. Here was, by the way, a case of that affinity that had so interested my preacher friend. This lady-like one had been a most successful hostess in New York, a model of charming manners, a great authority on good form; and now she was always being blown around with the soul of her butler. It caused quite a scandal.

I rather wondered that so many of these clever, charming women should be left drifting about. I think that, to begin with, they had wondered at it too. For they had travelled all over the world; there was nobody they did not meet, nothing they could not do (given the talent and understanding which one supposes, of course, they had). They were not used either to live in their big houses for more than a few months in the year. But perhaps, despite the wonders of the world they saw, and the glories of men's labour they glanced at and passed by, it was always the love of Fifth Avenue which was at the core of their hearts; so here they still are.

I did meet one most indignant party. He

took me (goodness knows why!) for a parson and attacked me straight away.

"Call this a future life!" he said. "It's disgraceful. You clergy ought to be ashamed of yourselves! No, never mind what denomination you belong to. You were all in a gang together. It was a regular religious Trust and you know it. Well, I put myself in your hands. Sunday after Sunday I sat under the most sensible one of you that I could find. I did what he said about giving money in charity and keeping well out of temptation. I believed all he told me; I squared the Bible with the higher criticism right along. I lived a decent life and I died without a murmur when my time came. And now I'm not a bit better off than I was before. What are you going to do about it?"

"But you must like it," I urged, for I was sure of my ground by this. "You couldn't be here at all unless you did like it, you know."

"It isn't a question of what I like," he persisted. "I didn't do things on earth because I liked doing them, but because they were the

Souls on Fifth

proper things to do. And when I made a firm contract I kept it. You chaps made a contract with me about a future state of bliss and I expect you to deliver the goods."

It was useless arguing with him. He had all sorts of minor grievances. He wanted the place kept more select. Not that he disliked all these other people, but he just thought they hadn't any right to be there. He wanted to know if his soul couldn't somehow be attached to his old house standing somewhere about Seventieth Street, which his widow and daughters still lived in. It would mark out a position for him, give him more dignity, he said. He even thought that his old room might be set apart for him and wouldn't I call on his widow and arrange it? But it was the general state of haphazardness that he most objected to.

"It's such a muddle," he grumbled. "I thought of forming a small well-chosen committee to deal with the problem. But there's no means of getting one together. And when I am blown up against anyone that might suit

Souls on Fifth

I find them absolutely selfish. Why that wonderful public spirit which used to animate us has not survived I cannot think."

"No," I said, "it is strange!"

He wanted me to form a committee on earth, was ready to subscribe, in reason, to its expenses if any means could be found of his doing so. He was sure that if the prominent citizens of New York could be brought to understand that Heaven was so near to them and was kept in such a condition they would see to its improvement at once, would remodel it, in fact, from end to end. He spoke of a travelling commission to visit similar future states in London, Paris, Berlin and Buda-Pesth.

"We could adopt the best feature of each," he said, "and I am sure that in addition our well-known efficiency and powers of organization would not fail us."

He was quite convinced that there was nothing either in the world or out of it which money and energy could not accomplish. I think he had been some sort of a business man.

Souls on Fifth

Then there was the soul of the painter that I found the wind beating frantically against the Metropolitan Museum. I asked him what in heaven's name he was doing there. He had been the forger, it turned out, of one of the most famous Old Masters in the collection. It was the best thing he had ever done. If he could have owned to it, it would have made his fortune.

I said I thought not, that what we wanted nowadays were new masters not old. But he would not listen to me; he was an academic soul. He had brooded on the wrong done him, on this theft of his genius that this snobbish flattery by the present of the past had committed, until his heart broke. He was sure, he said, that in a little while a kind wind would blow him into the Museum itself and up against his masterpiece and that then he would melt into it forever.

I have not said how strange the souls were to look at. Though their shapes did not answer at all to human shapes, yet by many curious variations they seemed to indicate character.

[33]

Souls on Fifth

I saw one once nearly five foot long and only a few inches broad, with curious markings all down. He was spiteful when I spoke to him. I don't know what he had been. Mostly, though, they were irregular ovals and oblongs about eight inches by three. There were rhomboids too and I saw several squares. At least, they looked quite square till you came to measure them up. There were some very tiny souls, some not larger than a dime; and there were some just scraps of rag, torn almost to bits; you wondered how they held together.

But it was the markings on them that were most curious. It was by these, even when they'd speak least about themselves, that I could often tell what they once had been. For as the thing you are in this world stamps itself in time upon your face, so will the things you do stamp themselves forever on your soul. Nearly all of them, for instance, had touches of rather tarnished gilt. One large and wobbly soul you might almost have mistaken for a torn bit of Russian embroidery, and one was covered with fine flowing lines

Souls on Fifth

like a Helleu etching. Some were warty; I never could bring myself to touch them. Many had holes in them and some were thick like little mattresses and plain dark grey. And when I had begun to learn the language of the signs, I found there were things marked upon some souls of which I cannot speak. They did not know that the evil thing was plain. They would talk to me as pleasantly and carelessly as you please. But while I listened to what they said I looked at what they were. There were the jagged lines that told of secret cruelties, stained blood-red into the souls of the torturers, whose homes had been but dungeons of despair for weaker souls than they. There were the white disease spots of the coward; mildew spots that rot away, in time, the very substance of the soul. There were the blisters of slanderous thoughts, which thicken and coarsen till the soul, a horny mass, is not sensitive to truth and love and beauty any more. No, there is no hell for such spirits. Is there any need for one?

Some souls, I saw, too, scored with the

marks of undeserved old suffering and loss.
These would sometimes look like well-healed
wounds, but with the women often they were only
painted and powdered down and I could see that
still they festered a little and were diseased.

It was in the very depth of winter that I
first found the Little Soul. The snow was
thick and crisp, the night dark, and the air
still. Mostly the rest must have been buried
deep; for nothing beats them down like snow,
and they have to wait for its thawing. But
she had been lucky and she hung to the branch
of a tree that bordered the park, for all the
world like a queer little grey icicle. I broke
her off, carefully, for she was frozen very stiff.
She would not say much to me that time. She
told me afterwards that she had been shy. But
I was quite used to that sort of thing though
indeed I had done her a kindness in taking her
from the branch and, when she had thawed a
little on my hand, letting her float up into the
calm air. I remember noticing chiefly that
she was very small (she did not overlap my
palm as she lay on it), of a pretty oval shape,

and light grey in colour; she had a slight silver down on her, shaded here and there.

Not more than two days later I found her again, at the extreme end of my beat this time, beyond the Reservoir. We talked for a while. She did not want to talk of herself, but asked much about me. This was the first time such a thing had happened with any soul. I told her that the end of my work was in sight and how I counted on leaving New York in a very few weeks for ever. Didn't I like it, she asked. I told her that I hated it, that I did not know whether I hated it more when I mixed in daytime with the people who thought they were alive or at nighttime with the people who knew they were dead. She said I was unfair, that it was a great city and she was sure there were still very charming people in it.

"That's it; it's not my business to be fair," I said. "New York is too big and I'm too small. But I can love it or hate it if I like."

She asked why I really hated it. I told her. It was a sufficiently good reason.

Souls on Fifth

She answered more readily now when I
questioned her about herself. She had died
young, at thirty-five or so; a bungled operation
which the surgeons could not own to. She had
been married to a quite well-known man,
whose name I had seen, curiously enough,
only a day before in the papers set to an an-
nouncement that he was marrying again. I
was not sure whether to tell her this; then I
did. She said she was very glad and asked the
name of the woman. I couldn't remember.

"Not that it matters," she said. "If she's
a reasonable sort of woman they should be
quite sufficiently happy."

"That is about the height of one's ambition,"
I said, "in making a second marriage."

After a pause she added, "I was quite happy
at least; I should have been foolish not to be."

"Did you leave any children?" I asked her.
"Stepmothers are much whiter than they are
painted, you know."

"No," she said. "I had three in the first
five years of my marriage. But one died
after two months and two were born dead.

Souls on Fifth

Then the doctor said I wasn't strong enough and forbade me to have any more. He couldn't make out why I wasn't, he had tried all the tonics he could think of. But I knew."

I waited for her to go on.

"It wasn't that I didn't love my husband or that he didn't love me. I think he did and he was always very kind. Though, indeed, people say that need not stop your having children; but I should think it would, shouldn't you?"

"Nature is not quite so nice," I answered.

She paused again. Then, unexpectedly — "When were you in the country last?" she asked.

I told her that a few weeks before I had gone for a walk on Long Island, how grey it had all looked and dead.

"But in a week or two," she said, "the woods will be wonderful. The green of the trees will almost pain you with joy, it'll be so sharp and bright. And there'll be dogwood that promises a happy year.

"I was born when the dogwood was in blossom," she said. "When I was little it was my birthday flower. On that morning mother always had them make an arbour of it for me. And after breakfast I'd be put there to sit in state and my presents would be brought to me. And when I died I know they put dogwood about my body and in my grave; that was in the springtime too. They thought it a pretty thing to do, but what did it matter then? Why, what had it ever mattered? What had that life and the beauty of it ever been to me from the beginning? Something I was taught to play with."

By now the barriers of my earthly state were down and she spoke on quite simply to my soul.

"But for all that I don't belong here, you know," she said, "drifting about above Fifth Avenue, and it's very dreadful. I never did belong here when I was alive, however happy I managed to be."

"Where did you belong?" I asked.

"In the wild places," she answered.

"Then why didn't you go to them?" I spoke crossly. I have no patience with people who talk helplessly.

Souls on Fifth

"Well, you see," she said, "my father was well off, and I was sent to school and brought out into society and married to the right sort of man. It was all done for my happiness. But always when my front door closed on me it was like the door of a cage closing. I was out of doors whenever I could be. I had a garden —"

"You had vegetables for dinner, I don't doubt," I interrupted.

"What would you have done then, had you been me?" she asked.

"Done what I wanted to," I told her.

"But when you can't want!" she said.

"Ah," said I, "there's no remedy for that."

"You see," she went on, "I was taught life like a lesson. I learnt it and I was repeating it, and then death came, and now it seems that I never even started to live. But is that why I'm never going to die? Because that's so dreadful."

This was new to me. "What more of that do you want to do?" I asked her.

Souls on Fifth

She cried out. "Oh, don't you understand? In Nature everything is so glad and proud to die — really and truly to die. To flower and fruit, to serve its turn, give what it is and has, then perish and be forgotten, not to cumber the memory of the earth at all. That's the true happiness, the only glory, to spend oneself utterly and die.

"I always hated having a soul," she said, "it made one so careful and egotistical. My flowers had no souls and while they lasted they were always fresher and finer than ever I was. My dog didn't have a soul to start with. He was a dear beast, quite undignified and foolish. Then, being so much in the house with us and what with the maids petting him, he began to grow a sort of imitation soul and became self-conscious and appealing. I sent him to the stables, I was so cross, and told them to train him after rats."

She laughed.

"You mean," I said, "that you never have wanted an immortal soul. Yes. I understand that."

Souls on Fifth

"What's the use of one?" she cried. "What's the use of all these silly shapes flapping around here? What good are they to themselves or anything else?"

"But what should happen to them?" I asked. "God never destroys anything utterly, you know. It's against the rules."

"I know what does happen," she said slowly, "to all the true lovers and workers who have given their strength without stint or question, without bargain or hope of reward, to the service that they saw. Their work is their immortality and the salvation of those they worked for and loved. For themselves they have earned oblivion. And if, their bodies dead, the fire of faith by which they burned like beacons in the dark does not at once die too, it falls in little flames of inspiration upon the hearts of all the comrades that could understand."

"That's a fine enough belief," I said, "and you put it so finely that I really can't make out what you are doing here at all."

"Nor can I," she replied, "and it's very dreadful, isn't it?"

Souls on Fifth

"Ah but I can," I added, and I told her coldly and hardly, as it had been truly told to me — "It is the things you do that count, not all the pretty beliefs and hopes, with which you decorate your heart and mind. The inexorable laws that God has made take no account of what you'd like to be and wish you were. How can they? What are you that you should complicate the scheme of things with Ifs and Ans? There's your life. Live it as you choose, and take the consequences."

She was dreadfully silent.

"But I didn't choose," she said. "And it's all very well for you! You haven't got to drift up and down this horrible Avenue for ever and ever and no amen. If I'd only known I'd have been wicked, so I would."

"Why wicked?" I was impatient.

"Yes, that's the silly thing," she said. "When you're so well brought up and well looked after you can't be yourself at all without being wicked."

I wondered how wicked she would have managed to be. And she caught me wondering before I was aware. We were slipping into sympathy, it seemed.

"Well," she exclaimed, "I was very pretty, I tell you I was."

I laughed. It's a paradox I always laugh at rather grimly. How can wickedness and the beauty of women go together? Oh, blindness of the morality of man! Then she went on to speak of other things.

When I wished her good-night she said: —
"You'll go back to those woods when it's springtime and the sun is shining through them, won't you? Go there in the early morning and sit silent and when the little live things around you begin to talk, think of me."

"I will," I said.

"For that was how my soul was meant to live and die, I'm sure," she said. "And it has never been itself since the Dogwood days."

For a week or more after this I did not see her. To say truth I did not altogether want to. I walked up the Avenue once or twice but I took care to keep her out of my mind and so, as I had begun to learn, kept her away

from me. For she had impressed me rather.
Not favourably; for all her fine thoughts her
chatter about wickedness showed her to have
been a frivolous little fool. But after the
struggles and temptations of some years I had
succeeded in detaching myself from all interest whatsoever in my fellow creatures and I
did not choose to be impressed, even unfavour-
ably, by anybody. The third time I went out,
though, I was making such conscious efforts
not to think of her that I only produced the
very opposite effect and there she hung in the
air a foot before my nose.

She was genuinely glad to find me.

"I began to fear we weren't in sympathy
at all," she said, "as you didn't turn up again.
By the way, are you a man?"

"Yes, of course," I told her. Somehow I
had assumed she knew.

"I couldn't be quite sure, you see," she
said, "only talking to you soul to soul. For
once we lose our bodies there are so many
gradations from malest-man to femalest-woman
that you can't always draw a definite line; and

sex in the old earthly sense doesn't seem to count. It's rather a blessing."

"Well, I am a man," I told her decidedly.

"I did put you down as one," she went on, "because you were so priggish the other night when I spoke of committing sin."

I denied being priggish.

"Oh, but you were feeling priggish," she insisted, "no matter what you said."

I told her she had no right to pry into my feelings.

"Nonsense," she cried, "you've the advantage of your body, you can run away when you like, leave me all the good I get from being a naked soul. I need never listen to lies again, not even little ones."

"Well, I do think that your notion of committing sin by running off with some man or other, or, worse, by not running off with him, was excessively trivial and vulgar. Besides, it wouldn't have kept you from being here. On the contrary."

I know that she smiled a little sadly.

"There it is," she said.

Souls on Fifth

"We don't want to go tumbling out of one man's arms into another's. Maybe you only encourage us to do it by calling it Sin. For what we do want is somehow to escape the terrible consequences of being good."

Then she moaned a little, sorry for herself.

"And I must, I must escape from this awful immortality," she said. "Isn't there any way it can be done?"

"Perhaps," I suggested, "if you could fix firmly in you a desire for something different it might be granted."

"No, we can achieve no new desires here," she said. "Isn't it dreadful?" That was a constant phrase of hers.

"Can't you call up the memory of an old one?" I asked. "There must have been something other than Fifth Avenue in your inner life."

"Now I'll tell you," she said. "I've tried that. I used to plan that when my husband got free of business, if he ever did, we'd take an old castle in Italy or on the Rhine and live there at least six months in the year. I fixed that idea well in him. He'll want to do it with his other wife now and I daresay she won't like it a bit. I wish you hadn't forgotten her name. Well, I thought to myself when I'd been dead a while : Half an eternity in any place in Europe is better than spending the whole of it here. So I set my desire hard on some old castle, just as I used to in life to make my husband promise he'd buy one. And one night I thought I'd got to it and I was so glad. There were the battlements and the rocks and the moonlit lake below. But it turned out only to be that sham place that's really the water-works in Central Park. So after that I gave up trying."

We stayed some time in silence. She had nothing else to say. I had no more suggestions. But we found, I suppose, some satisfaction in staying so. I was wearing a thick coat and leaning on the park wall; her soul was on my shoulder. Suddenly I said, "Good night. It's nearly dawn. I must be going."

"You said you might be leaving New York soon," she ventured.

Souls on Fifth

"Yes," said I. "And, quite unexpectedly, I'm through my work. I get off the day after tomorrow."

"Oh," she said, "good night," and never another word.

The next night I went out to say good-bye. I thought it would be only civil. I made no doubt we should find each other along that first half mile of park wall, that she'd descend upon me as she had done before. She wasn't there. I paced up and down, searching most carefully; my eyes were experts now. I spent the whole night searching. It was broad day when I stopped. I stood in the morning light with my face in my hands, fixing my thoughts in a final effort firmly on her. I hoped that, though I could not see, I should feel her presence near me if she came. Quite in vain.

I could not make up my mind to leave New York without seeing her. It sounds absurd, for what was she to me? What was she anyhow but a disembodied soul, one of thousands and thousands, and all past praying for, spite of anything the good Catholics may say. What

[50]

Souls on Fifth

could there ever be between us? My desires had certainly never been set on New York. Wherever I might find myself when I died it would certainly not be here. But I felt I could not go without seeing her.

For seven nights I searched from dark till daybreak, standing, willing her to come, pacing wildly, silently calling. I remembered then that I didn't even know her name. I slept exhaustedly all day.

On the seventh night the wind was rough. I was at the corner of Sixty-ninth Street when a gust blew her right in my face. I caught her and held her with the roughest grasp.

"Where on earth have you been," I said, "and what have you been doing?"

"I've been quite close to you lots of times," she said. "I can't make out why you didn't see me."

"Now don't you think that because I have a body I can be lied to either," I stormed at her, "you've been wishing yourself out of the way on purpose."

"Yes, I have," she said.

Souls on Fifth

"Why?" I asked her.

She did not answer.

"Will you tell me why?" I demanded.

"No, I won't," she said, "but if there's anything in it at all you ought to be able to tell without my telling."

"Well, I can't," I snapped.

"I knew you wouldn't," she said, "so what's the good anyway?"

"You really are a most irritating little soul," I said. "Will you tell me what it is you want of me?"

Not, poor dear, that she had shown she wanted anything. She made no answer.

"Will you please tell me what it is you want of me?" I repeated.

Still no answer.

"Then I shall wait here night and day until you do." I did not mean to be bullied. I had made up my mind to that.

A long silence.

Then suddenly — "I want to escape," she said. "I thought I was settling down to it, but talking to you has brought back Time again, and now when you go I shall want to escape worse than ever. I shall want to die and I shan't be able to. Won't it be dreadful?"

Her silly little phrase.

"But I really don't see what I can do to help you," I said. "If you can think of anything by all means tell me. I'll certainly try it."

"Where do you go to when you go?" she ,asked.

"I go West across the prairies and the mountains," I said, "and then Southwest across the sea."

"I knew that really," she confessed, "it has been in your mind all the time. I've been jealous of your having it so much in your mind."

"Well, go on," I told her, sharply, as my way was.

"I thought," she spoke slowly, "that if you could like me well enough to be able to carry me with you part of the way, then why shouldn't you leave me on the prairie as you passed? And there, if I fixed my desire on nothing-ness, the great wind might carry me to such a lonely place that I'd be almost as good as dead — really dead."

"We might try it," I said. "But you would have to like me enough to stop yourself flying back here."

"But how can I like you," she protested, "unless you like me first?"

"Like you in any ordinary sense of the word I certainly do not," I said. "I am a practical man. I have no use for these fantastic exercises of imagination. How do you expect me to like you?"

She sobbed aloud.

"That's because I've lost my body," she cried. "If I had my body back I'd make you like me fast enough — oh dear; oh, dear!"

I did my best to soothe her.

"And now I daresay I'm not even a decent-looking soul," she wailed.

I assured her she was a charming-looking soul.

"What shape am I?" she asked.

I assured her she was a perfect oval, and her colour a most delicate pale grey.

Souls on Fifth

"It sounds very dull," she said. "I've never dared ask anyone to tell me before. But compared with the others I suppose it's not so bad."

"But if I do try to take you, how am I to take you?" I asked her. "I can't carry you in my hand for two whole days. Besides in the daylight I'd lose you."

"Oh, but I've thought of that," she said. "What you want is a match-box to fold me up and put me in. No, not a real match-box, silly. But one of the — what used the spiritualists to call it? — one of the astral sort."

"And where does one buy those?" I asked.

I was sure she was smiling queerly.

"Have you never been in love with a pretty foolish woman?" she said.

"With dozens," I answered. I always say that; it is safer. But the fact is that I have never been in love at all.

She must have known both of the silly lie and the more shameful truth. But she did not remark on them. Instead —

Souls on Fifth

"Think of your love for a woman like that," she said, "and you'll find it very like a sort of match-box to carry me about in."

I never sleep in the train, so all night I sat upright in the darkened car. I had taken the Little Soul from my pocket and I held her against my cheek; and through the noise of the shaking of the train all night she whispered in my ear. She was sure she was going to die quite thoroughly now, she said, and did I mind her telling me things she had never told anyone before. "Why should I?" I answered her coldly. I was leaving the country; she could be certain they would go no further.

They were but simple things she had to tell. Of dreams, first for herself, then for her dead children, of little verses she had written and hidden and destroyed, of a temptation to unlawful love that she had shunned. Foolish things, I thought. And I stuck to the thought, though I knew she knew I was thinking it.

The next night I stood on the wide prairie and held her soul in my hand. It was late, for I had walked as far from the town as I could.

Souls on Fifth

There was no sound. It was cloudy and pitchy dark. No wind as yet, but a feeling as if a wind would rise.

"Now it's good-bye," I said. "I've kept my promise, and I'll wait, what's more, till the wind blows you away."

"Don't put me down for a minute," she begged. "I've something else to tell you."

"What is it?" I asked. "You were talking all last night."

"Oh, nothing about me indeed," she whispered. "I've nothing more to tell. But I wanted you to know why I told you about myself and didn't ask about yourself at all was only because, being so close to you, I could learn and feel and understand all there was in your heart. I knew all that you had done and suffered in your life from the beginning until now."

"Then you know of a poor thing," I said, "a black and hollow thing, a wasted thing."

"Yes," she went on. "And I knew that you were thinking that, but I wanted to tell you that I didn't think so at all. I think you've

Souls on Fifth

done very well in spite of what people call
your failure, and you've always tried your best.
Though fame has never come to you, you've
set your teeth and gone on, haven't you, and
never chattered or complained? And I wanted
to tell you that I love you for it."

"I never heard anything so ridiculous in my
life," I said. "How can you love me? We're
absolutely unsuited to each other in every way.
Not a tradition or a taste in common. Besides, you're dead. Quite dead in one sense
and almost dead in the other. What's the
use of talking about such things?"

"Now don't pretend to be cross when you're
not," she went on. "That's childish. I've
told you this for a very selfish reason. I
thought that instead of running the risk of
being blown about this great prairie for ever,
if you could learn to love me just enough
in return, my soul perhaps might pass utterly
into yours and in that way there would be
quite an end of me. Now don't interrupt me in
what I'm saying. You need a little something
like this added to you, a little common sense,

Souls on Fifth

a little patience, a little tenderness towards helpless things. You need it badly, and it's very conceited of you to pretend you don't. And, oh, my dear," she cried, and the very soul of her seemed to be throbbing. "Love is often like this, you know — how is it that you don't know? — Death to give, but always life to him that will dare take the offered love. And how gladly one dies to give it!"

"I do not love you," I said, "and I won't pretend to. I have never loved anyone and I never will. It's not worth it. I made up my mind to that long ago."

"Very well," she said. "It doesn't matter. Please put me down."

I put her down.

"Good-bye," I said.

"Good-bye," said she.

And then I knelt there for an hour or more. It was dark; I could not see her, and not another word did we say. Waiting so, I felt how dreadful eternity must be.

At last I heard it rise in the far distance, the northwest wind. Shaking and shrieking and rumbling it came, in leaps of gusty anger with silence in between. I set my teeth or I must have cried out in fear. But she made never a sound. Then it was on us, brutal, vindictive. I could not help it; I flung myself along the ground to shield her, groping with my hands where I thought she must be. My neck was bare and in a moment I felt the frail little thing she was fluttering close to me.

"I can't," she pleaded in agony, "I'm afraid. It's so cold and merciless and strong. I once had asthma as a child. Take me back to that selfish city. At least they'll understand me there."

"No, no," I whispered, "not back to that. That's worse than any hell. We musn't be cowards, we two, must we?"

"But I can't be lonely through eternity," she wailed. "I can't, I can't. It isn't fair to ask me."

Suddenly I began to shake as if a very ague were on me. I choked. I turned on my side for air. I crushed her soul between my hands. I ground it to my breast.

Souls on Fifth

I threw my face up to the dark above and a cry came from me that surely God Himself might have heard. "Oh, my dear little soul, my dear little soul!" And the ice within me broke and the tears sprang. I, that had not shed a tear since I could remember!

Before ever the tears could fall my hands that had held her were empty and my lips that would have kissed her foiled. The little soul had vanished.

But my soul was full of joy. And the wind, as I lay there, could not harm me nor the night make me afraid.

An Egyptian Love Spell

An Egyptian Love Spell

BY

MARIS HERRINGTON BILLINGS

NEW YORK
THE CENTRAL PUBLISHING CO.
CENTRAL BUILDING,
25 West 45th Street

Printed July, 1914

AN EGYPTIAN LOVE SPELL

CHAPTER I

IT was the week before Christmas. The glad
spirit of the season pervaded the very air,
as the crowds moved swiftly along. A
cheerful smile could be seen on most faces,
uplifted to watch the great snowflakes just beginning to fall in feathery whirls. The bright
raiment of the women was like the ever-changing
colors of the kaleidoscope, mixed with the more
somber clothes of the men. The one permanent
dash of color was the red-clothed Santa of the
Salvation Army, as he stood patiently ringing
his little bell, turning with a pathetic smile to
the hurrying crowds, hoping to extract a nickel

or dime from the charitably inclined. Many of those who passed turned back and dropped their coin into the wired kettle, hoping devoutly that no one would see them doing the kindly act.

Through this jostling, merry crowd, sauntered a young man. His handsome face wore a frown of disapproval as a pretty girl smiled engagingly upon him. The haughty and contemptuous look he gave her in return, warned the young lady with flirting propensities that this particular young man was not given to such frivolity. He sauntered on, thinking of the foolishness of pretty women in general.

While passing a jewelry store he gazed abstractedly into the window, and his eye caught the gleam of a ring of odd design; an Egyptian scarab made of green jade and surrounded with thirteen small rose diamonds, against a background of red and gold; it seemed to fascinate him. A sudden desire to hold it in his hand came over him. He entered the store, and the result was, he now had the ring on his little finger. The clerk was assuring him it was a great bar-

AN EGYPTIAN LOVE SPELL

gain at one hundred dollars: a real antique, taken from an ancient tomb in Babylon.

Long before he reached his cozy den in the bachelor apartments he occupied in Harlem, Jack was regretting the hundred dollars. He was without doubt a fool, he told himself, as he sank into the easy chair, before a glowing fire. The leaping flames shone on his handsome face, bringing into relief the black scowl that disfigured it as he meditated on his purchase.

Jack Drummond was now a youthful cynic. At twenty-seven the world fell short of his ideals. He did not believe in love. He was quite impervious to the charms of lovely women. He was above such sentimental trash; and there lay a letter from his chief telling him to write a love story. This was the last straw. It was absurd. He believed only in substantial facts; he never took pen in hand to write what he characterized as drivel. He took himself very seriously; and if he wrote of women, it was but to sneer at their little follies for which older men loved them. If the subject was men, he took pains to point out their vices, and forgot to mention the virtues of which we all have a small share.

He was looking into the fire as he watched the smoke curl in soft gray spirals from his glowing cigar; his thoughts were of his home in England. The son of landed gentry, he had irrevocably disgraced himself by being cashiered from the army, all on account of a pretty gaiety girl, who, at the last moment, had thrown him over for a millionaire, and left him a confirmed woman-hater.

He had then come to America, the Mecca of broken-hearted failures, to take up the severed strands and begin life anew. An old friend of his father gave the young fellow a chance on the staff of a New York daily paper, and he had turned out a fair dramatic critic. But to be told to write a love story, full of heart throbs, was the limit. His mind absolutely refused to work on such a subject.

Just at this moment his eye caught the gleam of the ring on his little finger. The inner side of the scarab was covered with hieroglyphics, which, to the initiated, meant the word "Besa."

AN EGYPTIAN LOVE SPELL

It was a beauty ring of ancient Egypt, sacred to the Goddess of Beauty, and worn perchance in that long ago by some beautiful maiden as a love charm. He had no idea that any significance was attached to a Besa ring; it was merely the odd design that had taken his fancy, and, now he possessed it, he wished he had his money back.

As he turned his finger this way and that, to note the sparkle of the tiny gems, he rubbed it lightly on his coat sleeve to bring out the scintillating gleams; then suddenly a strange thing happened. The electric lights went out, plunging the room into darkness. Jack noticed, it was not the ordinary darkness of night, for a soft silvery mist filled the room, and sitting quietly there in the midst of it, he had a curious sensation as of one beholding a vision. It was as if he were seated in a darkened auditorium and seeing a brilliantly lighted scene thrown on the screen before him.

Spread out before him, mysterious and indistinct, lay ancient Babylon. He knew it by the mighty walls that rose forty cubits in height, and wide enough to drive six chariots abreast. This wall surrounded a city of huge buildings and palaces and houses made of sun-dried bricks, with layers of rushes and palm leaves between each row. At intervals were gates of solid brass, ornamented with curious, fantastic designs, which represented gods, men, and winged animals. From each of the gates ran wide streets, which crossed each other at right angles; a beautiful stone bridge spanned the river Euphrates, which glided between the two great palaces.

Looming, vague and shadowy, like a ghostly giant, rose the Tower of Belus. This was the most wondrous structure in the city of Babylon. It was six hundred feet high, which is higher than the pyramids. It was built in eight sections, each one smaller than the other. Instead of stairs, there was a sloping terrace on the outside, wide enough for chariots and for sacrificial beasts to ascend. This great tower was sacred to the god Belus. The whole temple was adorned with idols of gods, for the Assyrians worshipped the stars as divinities. Nebo, Bel, and Ashtoreth, Queen of Heaven, were among the higher gods, while the sun, moon and the five great planets were supposed to time the inevitable march of the universe, which moved to the seven mysterious tones of music. Sacrifices and votive offerings were freely given to those countless stars that gem the southern sky under the title of the Host of Heaven.

Next to the temple was the old palace, strongly fortified. On the opposite side of the river was the new palace, with its pleasure-grounds and preserves, which covered a space of eight miles. Within this park were the celebrated hanging gardens, which consisted of terraces, one above the other, raised upon pillars higher than the walls of the city. They were first floored with cement and lead, then covered with earth, in which were planted most beautiful shrubs and flowers. It was a wilderness of myrtle and flowering almond trees, with here and there a dwarf cypress outlined against the sky. Only the music of the splashing fountains awoke the echoes in this sylvan paradise, fit abode for royalty during the heat of the Assyrian day.

Far out on the desert the golden sunbeams were shining with undimmed brightness. Across the sands moved a glittering procession, with the rearguard still below the sky-line of the desert. This array of stately spear-men, bronzed and scarred, were the famous horsemen of Assyria, returning from conquest. They were now within a day's march of the great city. The silvery notes of a trumpet sounded loud and clear, and the long line of camels and cavalry came to a halt with thankful hearts.

The brown tents were unrolled with lightning rapidity, only acquired by the daily repetition of such duties. Soon the desert was peopled with dusky tents, and banners fluttered in the heated air, while arms, accoutrements, animals and men seemed hopelessly mixed. Beasts of burden were wandering amongst bundles of unbound forage; spears were piled in sheaves amongst cooking utensils and drinking vessels; bows and arrows, shields, and habergeon were tossed indiscriminately on war chariots, horse-trappings, and scattered heaps of spoil.

Here was marshalled the flower of the Assyrian army, perfect in its equipment, formidable in its array when drawn up in solid phalanx to strike death and terror to the hearts of its opponents. In the shortest time the camp was reduced to order, and sounds of revelry rang from the great purple pavilion where sat the king, who loved this game of war. He was a fierce old warrior who loved to lead his armies into battle, mounted on the back of a noble steed encased in steel harness, following the great red banner on which was embroidered Merodach, the Babylonian god of war. Ninus asked no other favors of the gods. He pushed back the curtains of his tent, and smiled on his assembled soldiers. The great event was to take place—the division of the spoils of war.

Before entering Babylon, it was the custom of the king to bestow on his chosen favorites the maidens captured in battle. He was wont to present them as slaves to those whom he fancied most deserved the prizes, and great was the hilarity attending the ceremony. When that great host marched into Babylon, each man would boast of his treasure, and display the spoil he had won in Egypt; and proud was he that could show the greatest number of captives, fallen to his bow and arrow. There was great rivalry amongst the warriors, to pose before the women who came dancing out of the gates to meet them with timbrel and song.

The king was now about to reward his faithful allies; giving slaves to this favorite, to another a suit of mail or a talent of gold, or a span of those beautiful horses of stainless pedigree, prized for their matchless speed and grace of action; and many a warrior hoped the king would bestow on him these daughters of the desert, in preference to a dark-eyed maiden. The king turned to his shield-bearer. "Go bring the captive maids before me. I will set my seal of approval upon them," he said with a loud laugh.

Magon saluted and made his way to the quarters of the captives, where hundreds of poor wretches sat or stood drooping heavily in the heated air, their attitudes expressive of the utmost sorrow and despair. Yonder sat an Egyptian archer, gnawing his bonds in rage and cursing his Assyrian captors. There, a group of half-naked children huddled together asleep. A dark-eyed babe is stretching its tiny hands towards the tufted golden spears that mark the tent of royalty, while the dark-skinned mother gazes with dim and tearless eyes on the glowing sky. Over to the left stand picturesque Ethiopians whose gestures border on the grotesque. These men are so swarthy that they look as if cast in bronze, and the scowl of hatred with which they regard their conquerors is peculiar in its intensity. Their gaping wounds show that they have fought like demons before giving in to the victors. They were mercenaries attached to the army of Pharoah, and were caught in the successful raid of the Assyrians.

Apart from these stands a group of prisoners whose grave and quiet demeanor marks them with dignity and grace. They are loaded with chains.

Their white skins and flowing beards enhance the beauty of their dark eyes. They are Israelites, and keep entirely to themselves and accept the inevitable with a strange forbearance, but with a curious superiority; that they have knowledge and traditions far surpassing those of their masters. A white-haired patriarch is praying in their midst with solemn mien, addressing the unknown God of the Hebrews.

Magon makes his way to a group of young girls who cling to each other and shriek with despair, as they see the shield-bearer and his soldiers approaching. The soldiers select the younger women with practised eyes, despite their veils, and set them apart. But one, more fleet-footed than the rest, has flown to the old man and flung herself into his arms, where she makes frantic appeals to him to save her. Magon is young, and his heart fills with pity for the maiden clinging half fainting to her grandsire. He roughly takes a waterskin from a soldier standing near and tenders it to the old man, who begs her to drink. Magon draws nearer. "Fear not, oh daughter of Zion, I am pleading for thee, myself. Should my prayer be granted, I will guard thee with my life from all harm. Maiden, thou shalt be free as air," he whispered in a low voice. Then he took her gently by the hand and patted her reassuringly on the shoulder, while he led her, weeping, to the king.

The king sat on a great ivory chair, with his retinue grouped around him, his cup-bearer handing him wine with unflagging zeal. When Magon returned with the captives, he was careful to place Miriam as far in the rear as possible. The king ordered him to remove the veils of the maids. This many of them did without further ado. Ninus regarded those nearer him with a critical eye, shook his head at the plain ones, and nodded approvingly at those who possessed a fair share of good looks. Miriam was the last to be appraised. She refused to remove the embroidered veil. The king ordered Magon to tear it from her head. Obeying orders, Magon, gently but quickly removed it. The king saw a pale maid with hair of dusky hue, whose dark eyes were downcast. Her face had a look of profound sorrow. He shook his head dubiously, then laughed lightly as he turned to a fierce-looking warrior, saying: "By the god of Assur, methinks the lily-white maid would suit thee best, Phra."

Magon's heart was full of sympathy. He turned quickly and whispered to her: "Canst dance, oh maiden? If so, dance for thy life."

Miriam dropped to her knees, saying: "Oh, King, I am a dancer of Bubastis. May not my skill find favor in thine eyes?"

Ninus turned and ordered an attendant to bring a tambourine and men with harps. Miriam took the tambourine and poising lightly on one foot, she began to dance. She swayed as gracefully as a young palm bending in the breeze. She beguiled his thoughts, and he forgot for the time being that this was the distribution of the prizes.

When she stopped, he called a tall Nubian, and, nodding curtly, ordered her to be led away in an opposite direction from the other maids.

AN EGYPTIAN LOVE SPELL

Magon watched her as she passed the king's chariot. The heart of the shield-bearer beat with unwonted rapidity. On the long march from Egypt he had scarce noticed the maiden, she being of the captive race whom the Egyptians held in bondage, and whom the Assyrians despised. Magon knew that the Jews considered themselves a superior race, and scorned to mix with their conquerors or allow their children to intermarry with strangers. But when at the king's command he had roughly pulled aside her veil, he had been astonished at her beauty, and held speechless by her haughty glance. Something had passed from her eyes to his, and now he was the captive. In his heart a spirit had come to dwell, for good or evil. He had fallen in love with the Jewish maiden; and he sighed as his eyes followed her. She had danced divinely, and his Majesty had chosen to be well pleased. The graceful body swaying like a lily to and fro, to the melody of the tinkling harps, had soothed for the moment his savage soul, for Magon noticed that his piercing dark eyes still watched the retreating maiden. He refrained from asking the king to give him the captive at this moment, believing that after a few hours the fierce old warrior would in all probability forget that the maiden existed. But he was mistaken, for while the king's face bore an expression of habitual fierceness, heightened by his swarthy complexion, thick black brows, and curly beard, this old lion craved sympathy. Everyone with whom he came in contact dreaded him, and he longed for one human soul to treat him with frankness and frivolity. A strange expression passed over his grim old features; his face brightened; the blood rushed to his cheek; then he turned pale, and glanced at the bystanders with an air of inquiry. The wild joy of battle was over for the time being. For many a weary month in those long night watches, he had dreamed in his loneliness that when peace had come, he could find one human being to make its home in his fierce old heart. From his ivory throne he had noted the beauty of the maid, and out of the corner of his eye he watched the varying expres-

sions pass over the face of his handsome shield-
bearer.

With a scowl he turned in his chair. "Magon,"
he said, in such a loud tone that the shield-bearer
started involuntarily, "away to Babylon. Here,
Scribe, bring me a cylinder. Hear my message
to the queen and falter not by the way, or, by
the beard of Nimrod, I will compute the share
of the spoil I am likely to assign to thee, to your
especial entertainment on the altars of the gods."

Magon made low obeisance as he took the cylinder, leaped lightly to the back of his horse,
and rode away.

"Reach me that flagon of red wine," said the
king with a laugh to nobles of his circle, "I am
a good old sire in one respect—I pour all drink-
offering down my own throat. But what pleased
me most today, hath not been the great amount
of spoil, nor the glory of conquest, nor the empty
flatteries of those who surround me, but just the
face of a little maid sweeter than the rose, and
fairer than any maid in the land of Shinar.

CHAPTER II

THE sun was now on the decline. Its rays were flooding the desert. The sky was a faint green, tinged with streaks of orange and crimson, while the sands glowed like masses of molten gold.

On a superb Arabian charger rode Magon, who managed it with the grace and dexterity of youth; his dark eyes shining with a soft light, and his black curls falling in loose clusters on his tanned brow. He was arrayed in splendor. His armor, inlaid with gold, reflected the crimson rays of the sinking sun, so that he seemed to be enveloped in a mass of fire as he rode swiftly on. His shield was studded with precious stones, and from his left shoulder hung a mantle of crimson silk, broidered with heavy fringe of gold; even the heavy spear he carried in his hand was plated and ornamented with the same precious metal. The shield-bearer of the king was on his way to the new palace to apprise the queen of the near approach of her lord and master. Magon rode with the speed of the wind. Raising his spear, he passed unchallenged through the brazen gates, until he crossed the bridge, where he was met by a messenger from the palace, who had long awaited this horseman in shining armor. Magon proceeded with difficulty through the streets, until he came to a flight of broad marble steps, flanked by colossal bulls with eagles' wings and human heads. These were interspersed with gigantic lions with wings. These grotesque statues represented the Babylonian deities in mystic forms. On the gilded walls was painted in bright colors, a long procession of these strange monsters, such as were never seen on earth, in sea, or sky.

At length Magon was led into the presence of the Queen of Assyria, and prostrated himself at her feet. He dared not raise his eyes, for had he not heard that the queen was an enchantress, who could beguile a man's soul out of his body? He was aware of a strange, subtle perfume, like attar of roses mingled with incense, that seemed to pervade the air, causing a languid drowsiness to steal over brain and body.

"Rise, thou faithful messenger," said a musical voice. Magon sprang to his feet at the queen's bidding and stood before her, a rare specimen of manly beauty. His grace and bearing attracted her eye, and she gazed with admiration upon his handsome face. So he took courage to present on a silver tray, the brass cylinder covered with cuneiform writing, which held a scroll of parchment.

She gave him a smile and said carelessly: "Thinkest thou I am so dangerous to look upon that thou darest not raise thine eyes?"

"The light of thy countenance hath dazzled the eyes of thy servant," he said humbly.

"Nay, I would have thee look at me," said the queen. "Surely I can afford to be gracious to the trusty messenger that my lord hath selected."

AN EGYPTIAN LOVE SPELL

At these words, Magon ventured to scan the face and form of the celebrated queen, of whom he had heard so much, whose intelligence and beauty had made her a power in the East. She reclined on a couch of silver and ivory, and her beauty possessed a nameless charm that won men with a glance. Her form was matchless in its symmetry; every gesture represented grace and dignity. Possessing a man's power of mind and force of will, those bright eyes had the genius to command an army. Her hair was bright yellow, like rippling gold. Her eyes were greenish gray, and shone like two emeralds in the light of fading day. They were the most wonderful eyes he had ever seen, they not only won, but compelled admiration. Her exquisite face had the delicate color of a pink tinted rose, and bore the stamp of pride and resolution. In the curves of that rosy mouth and her well moulded chin, a close observer could detect the firmness that could carry out any wicked design her brilliant mind might plan, with stern implacable hardness, immovable as fate.

AN EGYPTIAN LOVE SPELL

But the comely warrior only saw a beautiful woman, who glanced with approval on him; and under the influence of her smiles, he began to expand, although the remnant of common sense he had left, told him it was well for those who served royalty to have no eyes, no affections, and no sympathy.

She was clad in a robe of golden tissue. The girdle of star-shaped ornaments which encircled her waist denoted her divine origin. On her fair hair rested a diadem of gold with an ornament in rubies and diamonds, representing an eagle's head encircled by the crescent moon. As Magon gazed on that lovely face, he doubted if she were human. Did she possess the same thoughts, the same passionate nature, as the women who followed the camp, and drew water for the herds? Nay, it could not be. Slaves were cast in a different mould from this divine one.

"Fear not to speak to me," she said softly, "for thou hast found favor in my sight. Henceforth thou shalt be my trusted messenger—what news of the host? Doth the king return in triumph, or doth his bones bleach on the burning sands?" Her accents were so pitiless, they made his blood run cold.

"The army hath returned victorious, most gracious Queen, with unlimited spoil and many captives," he answered shortly.

"Then my lord is safe, as usual?" she said with a rippling laugh.

"Hast thou won a captive," she said significantly; "and are the women of Egypt as fair as those of Assyria?"

"I thought so until I entered the Palace of Babylon. Now mine eyes have been dazzled by Ashtoreth. The sun hath blinded me, O Queen."

"Then let not the light that shineth in a maiden's eyes attract thee. I am pleased to accept thy homage; I am weary of compliments. Ashtoreth can bestow happiness on her worshippers, if they be earnest and discreet in their devotions," she said oracularly.

At that moment he felt death would be a cheap price to pay for a word or smile from those ruby lips, and his eyes did not fail to express his admiration. She bent towards him with a smile that was almost a caress, and bade him come nearer to her couch, while she glanced up at him with those wonderful eyes.

A thrill of pleasure went through him, as he marked her gracious mood; his heart was beating as never in the press of battle. His new taste for black hair and slender grace fled at the dazzling beauty of this regal creature, whose low musical tones seem to cast a spell over him.

She laid her white hand on his arm with a flattering gesture, and he felt the blood mount to his brain and the color to his cheeks at the thrilling touch. The male heart never becomes too old to respond to the flattery of a lovely woman, and his boyish vanity triumphed over his heart. He smiled, well pleased to have won the fancy of the great queen.

"Come to the palace tomorrow; thou shalt be a welcome guest." With these words she turned on him one of her rare, intoxicating smiles, and the young warrior left her presence dazed and confused, like a man waking out of a dream.

AN EGYPTIAN LOVE SPELL

Now as he walked under the stars, he began to think how dangerous it was to have taken the fancy and pleased the eye of the queen, for he knew it were wiser to trust himself to the winds of the khamsin than to question the caprices of a wilful woman, and more, the one who wore the diadem of Assyria.

As he hurried through the wide streets of Babylon, before his eye there arose a vision of a delicate face with rich southern coloring and jet black curls, and great serious brown eyes. What was she doing now, the captive maid? In a few hours at most, she must reach this great city. What fate did those shining stars hold in store for her, and for him?

CHAPTER III

THE sun had scarce risen, gilding the towers of Babylon, when the trumpet awoke the echoes and the long line began to move like a huge snake. As the king left his tent, wearing his heavy harness, the vast host was set in motion. From his attire none would dream that the silent man, sitting astride the great war-horse which snorted and plunged with a force that would have unseated many a younger man, was the mighty King of Assyria. He wore neither diadem nor crown. Only a steel helmet, much dented and battered, covered his locks. His shield was plain and badly defaced by sword and spear thrust. His dress and the trappings of his horse could not compare with those of his bodyguard; but he was accounted the bravest soldier and the greatest warrior of his time. He was followed by a body of horsemen glittering in scarlet and gold, raising clouds of dust, as their horses neighed and pawed impatiently. Then, with measured tread came a long line of spears, carried by stalwart warriors, weather browned and bearded; then the war-chariots, a thousand in number, with a roll like distant thunder as the massive wheels tipped with iron sank deep in the sand; then came the drooping, listless captives, guarded on every hand, marching with dragging footsteps. Linked together with heavy chains on their shoulders, they carried sad eyed children or heavy burdens of treasure, and household goods, all the spoil of the victors. The women tore their hair and wailed in anguish, while some fell on their knees and implored their impassive guards to kill them with the gleaming cimeters that hung at their belts.

AN EGYPTIAN LOVE SPELL

In the midst of these poor drudges was a richly gilded palanquin with purple hangings embroidered in gold, borne by four ebony-faced Nubians, and among its silken cushions sat Miriam and her grandsire. She was thanking the lucky star that she had drawn the attention of Magon to her miserable plight; her thoughts dwelt steadily on his kind eyes; her heart filled with gratitude to the Assyrian whose standing at Court made these comforts of the journey possible, not dreaming that 'twas by the orders of the king she was thus singled out and favored.

CHAPTER IV

O N the first night in Babylon it was the
custom of the queen to receive her con-
sort and his chief officers at a great
state banquet given in honor of the
return of the warriors from conquest. The king
had been in the saddle since day-break. He was
weary with the endless ceremonials, the sacrifices
to the gods and the posing before the people.
Turning to his master of ceremonies, he said:
"I am weary; bid the music play, and have the
Jewish captive dance; for my tired brain seems
soothed to slumber as I watch her flying feet.
Oh, great Babylon, to be once more within thy
walls, after all these months of marching across
the burning deserts. 'Tis well, to behold peace,

plenty, revelry, wine and women," he said with a sigh of relief.

At this moment the music burst forth in a weird melody and the slim little dancer entered, clad in a robe called a sindone, a species of fine tissue, delicate in texture, of a pale nile green color, and worn only by royalty. It was embroidered in threads of gold; and she wore a wreath of white lotus flowers on her dark hair.

A storm of applause greeted the performance of the maiden who had found favor in the eyes of the king, and she retired amid a shower of flowers which the guests tore from their wreaths and threw at the feet of the slave.

But 'twas with a heavy heart that Miriam crossed the great courtyard, for she had to pass the band of captives, her own people, huddled together like sheep. In the center of a group apart from the rest stood her grandsire praying aloud in the unknown tongue. His stately bearing and exalted attitude attracted Magon, who beckoned to his side a slave bearing food and wine.

"Comfort thy heart, O prisoner," he said, "I will see that thy fetters are removed at daybreak if the king feels in a gracious mood."

Reuben looked upon Magon with mild and condescending pity. "Canst release the maiden from the claws of the lion?" he said scornfully. Magon could not help but admire this chief of a nation of slaves.

"Thou dost offer me wine and bread. It shall be returned to thee a hundredfold," he said with grave dignity.

"Dost think the gods will reward me?" said Magon with a laugh.

"Our fathers have taught us so to believe," said Reuben. "Although I stand here a captive, I protest against your temples, your idolatry and your worship of the beasts. You have no right to degrade the worship of the Omnipotent One."

Magon smiled indulgently.

"Thou dost forget the stars. They are the chosen divinities. Thou canst not form a nobler ideal of gods, spirits, heroes, what you will, than those silent glowing orbs of light. Art thou a mystery-teacher among thy people?"

"Nay, it needs no mystery for our worship. It is clear as the light of day. The one God rules in the eternal heavens."

"The mighty Ashtoreth, Queen of Heaven, presides over our destinies."

"Nay, I speak not of man-made gods. The time will yet come when all shall worship and bow the knee to the one God alone. He shall bring all the nations of the earth to his feet. For awhile Babylon seemeth to prosper; but she shall perish and pass away, as a flower that is cut down."

"Ah, thou hast the power of divination. Didst learn the art amongst the Egyptians? They boast of their proficiency handed down through a score of generations. Come, tell me out of thy lore the fate that lies before me. Shall I mate with the eagle or the dove?"

"My lore thou wouldst deem beneath thy understanding. It consists of but one sentence:

Do justice, love mercy, and deal with men as if thou were going to face thy God."

"And thou art a slave. I would that Ninus might hear thee converse; perchance he would learn wisdom of thee."

"I would that he would let Miriam toil under the lash of the taskmaster, than have her quartered there," said Reuben sadly, pointing to the grim pile looming shadowy and indistinct on his right. "Some day I feel that we shall be free. Retribution will overtake the Egyptians. They shall enter the home of bondage. They shall eat the bitter bread of slavery. They shall weep tears of blood under the goad of the taskmaster's lash. Some day our God shall surely free us, for are we not the descendants of his chosen servant? The day will come when the oppressed shall rise. The Children of Israel shall throw off the yoke of the oppressors, and be free as the birds of the air."

"Dost expect a king to come with rolling of chariots and blowing of trumpets, riding on the wings of the western wind to rescue thee, O slaves!"

"Aye, Assyrian, I do expect a mightier king than thine, who shall lead us forth from captivity."

Magon laughed heartily. "In the meantime, thou hadst best refresh thy inner man with what the Babylonian gods provide for thee," he said lightly.

But Reuben only moaned in a low tone. "O, Miriam, Miriam," he wailed in a long-drawn note of agony and despair. The sound was taken up by the others and was repeated again and again, causing the king to rise up in his wrath and vow that every one of the sorrowing herd of captives should die at break of day, until he remembered one had found favor in his sight. And fain would she be among them, but the eunuch had hurried her along to the building where the slaves were quartered. The Host of Heaven in all their glory, shone down in their eternal splendor on the pomp and magnificence of the royal court of Babylon.

CHAPTER V

'TWAS now verging on midnight. The king and queen had gone to their respective palaces. Magon stole away from the revellers and made his way to the hanging gardens where brooded the solemn hush of night. The wild birds had long sought their nests, and the graceful deer reclined in the dark shadows that lay across the smooth green turf of the surrounding preserves. The dim recesses of its silent groves were bright as day, for a full moon shed its silvery light over the beautiful scene. The sight of the little dancer amidst all the splendor of the court had aroused Magon's protective nature. What could he do to show her she had a friend at Court? He thought of that long journey across the deserts, the danger, the privations; they were as nought to him, and only served to stir his blood to wild adventure. Better a goat's hair tent in the wilderness with him than be a favorite of the fierce old king. Far better her talent had not been discovered, and she were the meanest slave, drawing water for the herds and camels, than living in a palace of gold. She had crept into his heart unawares. He was determined to see her this very night, tomorrow might be too late. Nay, he would talk with her this very hour, before the gods had time to cast his own lot beyond recall. He hurried through the shadows of the sleeping gardens, for the king's shield-bearer could pass unmolested by the guards. On he went to the great brick building, where the dancers were quartered.

Outside its grim walls, he paused, and, softly imitating the call of the murkowis, or ring dove, calling to its mate, he waited.

Magon was trained to warfare. He reviewed all sides of the question. He took into careful consideration the important doctrine of chance. He suspected, and with good reason, that the queen had taken a fancy to himself—it was flattering to his self love—for there was no mistaking her interest and her obvious condescension. "But methinks a two-edged sword is oft carried in a scabbard of velvet and gold. I would be more than a fool to trust to the honeyed words that fall from the lips of the queen; a burning sigh will not protect me from her changing moods. Rather shall I choose this ice maiden; but her people neither give in marriage, buy nor sell, their maidens. I wonder what she will say," he mused.

In a short time a little, graceful figure glided like a pale ghost from beneath the shadow of the tower, and flitted past him in the moonlight. Magon followed discreetly, as soon as he had made sure that no eye but his had seen that ghostly form.

Plunging into the shadows he came up with her. "O, Queen of my heart, thou hast risked thy life to answer my call; but I must ask thee, art thou willing to trust me? I will take thee away from the palace. I know where I can hide thee, and tomorrow eve we will away across the sands to Palestine."

"I would that we could, my Lord, but a Jewish maiden, according to the laws of our people, cannot mate with an Assyrian. But, alas! our hearts are wayward, and all the laws ever made cannot stay our hearts from loving; and I love thee. I knew full well that thou wouldst try to see me tonight, for thine eyes did tell me so," she said shyly, hiding her blushing face in the folds of her veil.

"Then, mount my good war horse and fly into the desert with me," he responded promptly. "Let us enjoy the good things of life, while we may. Life is short. Death is long. Ere the sun sets, the lotus will fade; the mood of the king changeth with every wind that blows."

He looked at the beautiful girl beside him, the very contrast of her flushed face appealed to him. Every manly instinct in his nature rose to protect this helpless slave. He found he loved the little maid with all the warmth and stormy passion of his race and climate.

AN EGYPTIAN LOVE SPELL

"Let us defy the laws and royalty," he whispered. "We can die but once." And he folded her in a loving embrace. "What can I do to prove to thee that I love thee better than life?"

"Naught, just now," she said, smiling up at him, "but I will prove to thee how much I love thee. See! This is my Besa ring; 'tis charmed. Canst read the inscription? It was given to me by an Egyptian priest, who told me that if I parted with it I should sacrifice the dearest wish of my heart; that love, happiness and life would leave me; that the one to whom I gave it would gain those gifts; and, that its power would be lost to me until once more it should be placed upon my finger by the one I love."

"Dear heart! if thou believeth what is written in the stars, then thou shouldst be more careful of thy priceless charm. I would not deprive thee of it for a moment of time. I wonder if the amulet controls destiny; or is it destiny that gives value to the amulet?"

"I know not, dear one; but we shall see." With that she slipped the ring on the little finger of his right hand. As he drew her close to his heart, she whispered: "I would be quite willing to pay the price," and she hid her face on his shoulder. Then suddenly he felt her shiver from head to foot, and she grew deadly pale in the moonlight. There was a thrill of fear in her voice as she whispered: "O Magon, pity me, save me! What shall I do? Methinks I saw the green eyes of the queen gazing upon me from yonder bushes."

"Nay, nay, dear love, thy fears doth run away with thee; but still it were best to fly, for 'tis said she walks like the leopard, by night, in this, her favorite retreat," and, pressing her hand hastily to his lips, he watched her glide swiftly into the shadows.

As she disappeared he drew a sigh of relief and stood motionless as a statue; his heart was beating wildly, for now he could plainly hear a soft, measured tread and the rustle of a woman's garment. He turned his head, and there stood the queen. Trembling in every limb, Magon prostrated himself on the marble walk at her feet.

AN EGYPTIAN LOVE SPELL

"Arise, Magon," said the soft purring voice of the queen, "wert thou worshipping the stars when I approached thee?"

"By the beak of Nisroth, I was but thinking of thy divine self, your Majesty," he answered with ready wit. But her eyes narrowed to a mere slit, and her fair face became rigid. Such a gleam had Magon often beheld in the eyes of the king when condemning some poor wretch to death.

"If thou canst read the stars, perchance thou canst see thy destiny written there. I am glad to see thou art on guard in my garden; thou hast managed well; thou art in truth a courtier as well as a soldier. Thy Queen is gratified to know thou art here; thy thoughts cannot fly too high. Magon, aspire to the highest. Ashtoreth, Queen of Heaven, smiles on thee at this moment."

"I believe that man makes his own destiny," whispered the Queen, softly. "He can rise to great heights or sink unknown, according to the woman he chooses."

AN EGYPTIAN LOVE SPELL

She glanced keenly at his face, then she walked slowly away, following the winding path, grave and abstracted, as though weighing in her mind some mighty matter of state.

Magon stood looking after that superb figure, his heart sick with horror of the narrow escape he had from being actually caught caressing the little captive. Nay, it was impossible. The queen could not have seen her, for Miriam had fled fully two minutes before he had heard even the rustle of her garments, or the footsteps of her attendants. Thus to himself did he speak; for alas, he felt very weak. "Methinks the desire of the queen is like the hot winds of the desert. Death doth follow in its wake," he said with a sigh.

The queen went to her gorgeous apartments, where scattered around were costly articles of furniture, ivory couches covered with the skins of lion and leopard, silken cushions and tables of elaborate Egyptian carving. She seated herself in a gilded dipros, and bade her handmaiden take down her hair, which covered her like a fleece of gold. Presently she spoke, in a languid tone, saying: "What maiden wore a pale green sindone tonight?"

Her attendants looked at each other and trembled. At last one ventured to say: "The Babylonian robe hath been bestowed, O Queen, on one of the captives, a Jewish dancer, who hath found favor in the eyes of the king."

"Ah, so! The wind bloweth that way," said the queen musingly. "She hath made the long journey across the desert, and hath more than a winning way."

She clapped her hands, saying to the black eunuch who answered the call: "Bring the Jewish dancer before me, Benoni."

With a wave of the hand she dismissed her attendants, and in a short time the Nubian returned, leading Miriam into the dread presence of the queen, who surveyed the trembling maiden with a scornful curl of her lips.

She looked her over from head to foot, and said with a sneer: "Thou poor grey linnet, methinks thou wilt be better off in a cage, lest the eagle soaring through the limitless ether take a fancy to thy dun grey plumage."

Miriam glanced up at the rosy, smiling mouth, at that beautiful face, and noted with growing terror the cold, pitiless gleam in those brilliant eyes.

With indolent grace the queen moved her chair, rubbed her dainty foot across a carved ornament set in the floor, and behold! the great marble slab began to slide back, disclosing to view a black, yawning pit. With a gesture, the queen commanded the eunuch to lower the girl therein. As he obeyed, she said coldly: "If thy moans and howls disturb my slumbers, I will send thee a couple of scorpions to keep thee company."

With that she touched a spring and the slab rolled silently into place; and the queen lay calmly down upon her silken cushions and fell asleep.

CHAPTER VI

THE following evening when the sun was filling the western sky with glory, the queen sat before her burnished mirror. "Tire me well. I would win all hearts," she said with a laugh. "I would make an impression tonight. Aye, I will tell him I know the maiden is safe—that I have given her into the arms of a lover who will hold her forever," she said to herself. "Does he think to deceive me? But yestereve I bade him hope, and he went to that sickly slave for comfort. Now he shall feel the weight of my power. Shall I send him to keep her company? Nay! I will crush him as I would a worm; his heart shall grow cold, longing to know whether the slave has been sacrificed to the gods or to an earthly lover."

AN EGYPTIAN LOVE SPELL

As she gazed at that faultless face and form reflected in the mirror, not an eyelid quivered, nor did her jeweled hand even tremble as she smoothed her fair hair. She was hard and white as marble. In that bosom no pity entered for the fair blossom lying in a crushed and helpless heap beneath her gilded chair. Semiramis had come in contact with a man who had dared resist her charms. His preference for the slave had aroused her worst passions. As she sat there with her rippling hair of gold and those marvellous eyes, she reminded one of a leopard, for her robe was of cloth of gold embroidered with black sequins, and her expression was the same as the green-eyed, cat-headed goddess Sekhet, worshipped by the Egyptians at Bubastis. She was now determined to bring Magon to her feet for the mere sake of conquest and the gratification of her own desires; then he should die. There are some women whose passions are like a consuming fire, and it were well not to arouse them.

Now as the evening began to wane, the fierce

old king thought more than once of the new dancer. As he sat on his throne, his face lightened and the scowl fled, when the musicians began to play the familiar tune. He looked up with a smile, but a dark-skinned maid from Arabia was dancing, then came a fair-haired, blue-eyed dancer from Lybia—famous for generations for her dancers at the court of Pharaoh.

"Now bid the Jewish maiden dance," he said with a wave of his hand. "From this moment she is free. She is my chosen acherra."

The master of ceremonies fell at his feet. "O, Sire, naught can keep the evil tidings from thine ear. The Jewish maiden hath disappeared from the palace. Perchance the gods have spirited her away, for none in Babylon hath beheld her this day."

For a moment the king spoke not a word. Then his eye fell upon his shield-bearer, who stood stunned at the news. The king became very angry. Had Magon dared to aspire to the maid?

"Magon," he said in a voice of thunder. The

soldier saluted and prostrated himself at the feet of the irate king. "Knowest thou aught of the Jewish captive?"

Magon's tongue clove to the roof of his mouth. He could not answer for sheer terror as he thought of her probable fate. At length he stammered: "Nay, I swear by the Seven Stars that I know naught of the maiden, nor her whereabouts, nor have I seen her this day, O great King!"

"Thou liest," said the king, eyeing the young warrior, sternly; for Magon's confusion was plainly visible to all assembled.

"By Ashtoreth, this is too much," said the king, springing to his feet, his voice shaking with ungovernable rage. "I believe thou art lying; not only hast thou seen the maiden, but thou hast helped her escape from Babylon. Ho! guards, away with him. He shall pay the penalty; let him die at sunrise. Cover his face and lead him away.

At this moment the queen entered the great hall, and her keen eye noted the guards dragging

Magon away. She raised her eyebrows with just the faintest flicker of surprise, for she had heard that stentorian command even in the outer court, but knew not who it was that was being led forth to die. She passed swiftly to the foot of the throne, and lifting the king's sceptre she kissed it in token of submission, while she veiled her blazing eyes.

"Your gracious Majesty, dost remember 'tis thy natal day, the day on which thou art wont, as a rule, to extend mercy to those who offend thee. Spare then, I pray thee, thy shield-bearer, O King."

"Nay," said he with a frown. "His offense is one I will not overlook. I have spoken."

His beard was bristling with rage and a red light gleamed in his eyes. When the king looked like this, it was vain to sue for mercy.

Ninus arose, a set look of determination on his face. Magon should die, but not before the torturers should wring from him the place where he had hidden the rose that it had pleased the king to take. He was an imposing figure as he descended from his throne, arrayed in all his robes of state. Around his shaggy curls of grey hair, gleamed a diadem of gold. His long flowing garment of silk was embroidered in mystic symbols, and edged with a fringe of gold. His mantle of violet silk trailed behind him, and his long muscular arms were bare, save for the golden bracelets that twined like serpents round them. His feet were encased in sandals of gazelle hide strapped on with gold bands.

"Tomorrow," he muttered, "tomorrow we shall see whether the lion shall be robbed by a cub." Then he withdrew behind the heavy folds of a velvet curtain, that led to his private apartments.

No sooner had the soft folds fallen into place than the queen crossed the room with quick, graceful steps. Taking in her hand the jeweled flagon Ninus habitually used, she held it out to the cup-bearer.

"May the king live forever. Pour the libation. Verily the wine must have lost its savor. My lord hath forgotten his midnight draught.

Tell him I provide it with humble devotion ere he goes to slumber.'

Turning to those assembled she raised it to her lips, then held it on high. Then, turning round, she passed her right hand over the cup. She watched the wine boil and bubble with a smile. Again she held it aloft invoking the gods.

"Go bid my lord drink. Tell him I wish him all success. May his heart's desires be granted," she said with a mocking laugh, as the page followed the king to his room.

An hour later, the queen entered that vast chamber. Lying in a deep slumber reposed the king, his trusty dagger on the floor beside him. She regarded with disgust the recumbent figure, for the drugged wine held him chained to the couch. She watched him with peculiar feelings. She longed for him to die, to give her an opportunity to reign in his stead. She turned her eyes away from the dagger lest she make sure.

"A fig for thy threats," she said, snapping her fingers, as she knelt down, and with practised hands abstracted from beneath his pillows a large golden seal, attached to a chain round his neck. This she slipped off with ease, tossed her head, cast upon him a haughty and contemptuous look, and swept from the room.

She made her way to her own apartment, where she dismissed all but her favorite attendant. This done, she gave her orders; from a hidden recess in the wall, the slave girl took a complete suit of armor. In the queen's heart a sudden revulsion had taken place. She would torture Magon herself, but the king should not rob her of her prey. Now she would risk all to protect him. She feverishly stripped off her garments and donned the suit of mail; breast-plate, helmet, greaves, all complete. Taking the sword from her attendant she pointed to an ivory settee. "Await my coming," she said imperiously, and left the room.

Through the dim corridors, a slim young warrior in shining breast-plate and helmet, with a face like Shamash, the god of light, was seen to pass the guards, to whom he presented the king's own signet, and he entered unchallenged the cell of the prisoner.

Magon looked up astonished at this bright vision, then prostrated himself at the feet of the warrior, for he recognized it was none other than the queen.

"See how I forgive thy infidelity. I have come to save thee," she said brokenly. "Outside the walls is waiting the swiftest dromedary in the land of Shinar. Fly to my own citadel of Ascalon. There thou shalt be safe in the city of refuge. I would that I might join thee there."

She looked tenderly down on the kneeling figure at her feet, leaning towards him with the graceful pliancy of a young palm bending in the evening breeze. And even the love and longing for Miriam which burned in his heart, could not subdue the passionate admiration he felt as he gazed into the eyes of the loveliest woman on earth.

"Rise, Magon. This is no time for homage."

Meeting his glance, her own wayward heart kindled into fire. She laid her hand tenderly on his shoulder with a gesture that was a caress. "I have come to save thee," she said softly. "I could not let thee die like this. I give thee thy life as a free gift. Thou leavest behind thee a queen, forsooth, who thought to love and cherish thee; but the gods have interfered in our love-making, for in the moment I gained thee, I lost thee as well."

Magon sprang to his feet. "O Queen, I have but one desire; to live and die at thy gracious feet."

" 'Tis well," she said, "come; I now bid thee ride for thy life to the city of refuge. Farewell, Beloved! Perchance I shall yet visit my citadel," and she glided away, followed by the shield-bearer.

She let him out of the brazen gates with her own hand, and the sunrise saw him leagues from Babylon, and well on his way to Ascalon.

* * * * * * *

Now the scene changed, and before Jack's astonished eyes was the stage of the Hippodrome with its gorgeous ballet, the dancing figures moving swiftly, like the changing colors in a kaleid-oscope, and, conspicuous among them, to his great surprise, he saw Miriam, the captive maid of Babylon.

The orchestra was playing a soft, dreamy melody. Every pair of hands in the big auditorium was clapping a warm welcome to the little dancer; her eyes were like stars; her dusky cheeks like the petals of a rose. One could see that she was very happy; she loved her art; it filled her life; the sound of the music, the applause of that vast audience satisfied her. The one great wish of her heart was that she might some day dance before a crowned head; and she hoped that it might be a fierce old king, with a kindly smile. If she could only dance before that old tyrant, she felt that the supreme moment of her life would come, and then only would she be mistress of her art.

Jack seemed to know this intuitively, and watched the scene as if fascinated. Then suddenly the silvery mist faded away; the electric lights went up, and Jack rubbed his eyes in amazement, as he glanced round his familiar rooms. "Good heavens! have I been dreaming?" he said, in a bewildered way, "or was it an optical illusion?"

The next evening found this cynical young man at the Hippodrome just to satisfy himself that the vision he had seen was not a mild form of indigestion. Seated in the second row of the orchestra Jack saw that every detail of that ballet had been faithfully reproduced in his room. At the first bars of the music that preluded the third act, he knew he should see Miriam in that shimmering robe of pale green tissue. She came on in a triumphant burst of music and danced down to the footlights. She saw him; their eyes met and they looked at each other in a long strange gaze. She nearly lost her step, and shivered visibly as she glided into the wings.

After the performance she was not surprised to see the tall stranger talking to the manager; and a few moments after she was bowing to him. While a conventional introduction was being spoken, her heart was beating wildly as she heard him say:

"May I have the pleasure of a few moments' conversation with you? Miss Darrel, may I present you with a little trinket that I think once belonged to you in the long ago?"

"How strange," she murmured. "How do you know it belonged to me?"

"I know that when you parted with it you lost your life, love and happiness, all that made life worth living; and I have a fancy to return to you again that ancient charm—your long-lost Besa ring."

He held out to her the ring and she slipped it on her slender finger saying softly: "I was told not long ago that I should receive a gift that once belonged to me in a former life, and that it possessed the power to bring me love, protection and perfect happiness."

"I am quite certain it will," said Jack gallantly. "You once gave that ring to me, and I now return it with my love. If you could only take the donor as well as the charm," he said

AN EGYPTIAN LOVE SPELL

ruefully, "then the romance would be complete."

And Miriam, looking up into the dark eyes so quizzically looking down, replied: "Time makes no difference in our innate philosophy. With the Moslems of the East, I say, why not! Allah is great! 'Tis his doing! Kismet! You and I are but instruments in the hands of fate. I feel sure we belonged to each other in the long past. So why oppose fate?" she said with a roguish smile.

And Jack Drummond, who sneered at love, agreed joyously it was useless to fight Kismet.

"Come," he said tenderly, "let me prove that your confidence is not misplaced. Let me tell you the story of my love in Babylon."

THIRTY PIECES OF SILVER

[See p. 20

THIRTY TIMES DID A PIECE OF SILVER DROP INTO THE OUT-
STRETCHED CLAW

THIRTY
PIECES OF SILVER

BY
CLARENCE B. KELLAND

ILLUSTRATED

HARPER & BROTHERS PUBLISHERS
NEW YORK AND LONDON
MCMXIII

ILLUSTRATIONS

THIRTY PIECES of SILVER

ORDINARY men and women made up Carnavon's audience—shopkeepers, artisans, doctors, lawyers, clerks; and he held them breathless, spellbound. They leaned forward in their seats, every one of the two thousand of them avaricious of each vibrant word. In obedience to his genius they swayed with laughter, rewarded his pathos with tears, gasped at the daring of his climaxes. And yet he attacked

1

what many of them held most dear—their God.

From the instant of Carnavon's appearance on the platform the audience had been his, conquered before he uttered a word by the potency of his presence, by the excellence of his physical self, by the magnificence of the animal. At his first utterance there seemed to arise a collective sigh, and thenceforward until he ceased speaking his hearers were not their own, but Carnavon's.

The showman moves his puppets with invisible threads, so that they dance and posture and contort themselves as he wills; Carnavon's invisible threads reached not from his fingers to the limbs of his audience, but from his mind to their brains and hearts — and they comported themselves according to his desires. He was such an orator as the world hears once in many generations. He held sacred matters dangling before men and women in whom religion had been planted and watered from the cradle, yet under his relentless logic, his flashing wit, his acid irony, they shriveled and crackled to ashes and were sacred no more. Out of curiosity, men firm in their faith came to see and hear him; they departed doubting God, if not denying Him; groping for a foothold in a world he had deprived of its firm foundation.

This thing Carnavon did for a price—for one thousand dollars a lecture.

After his address Carnavon was driven to his hotel, and went at once to his apartments. Scarcely had he made himself comfortable, with a book to compose himself before retiring, when a knock sounded on his door. He closed his volume impatiently.

"Come in," he said.

The door opened reluctantly, and Carnavon was startled to see on his threshold an old man—embarrassed, hesitating—an old man white of hair, with patriarchal beard, clothed in the garb of the Salvation Army.

"Mr. Carnavon," he said, diffidently, "may I come in?"

Carnavon recovered himself and motioned to a chair. "How can I serve you?" he asked, rising with always ready courtesy.

The old man paused a moment before replying, and fumbled the vizor of his cap.

"You can give a few of the many

4

AN OLD MAN—EMBARRASSED, HESITATING—IN THE GARB OF
THE SALVATION ARMY

minutes yet before you to an old man whose course is nearly run," he said at length, and his voice was singularly gentle, "a few minutes leavened with patience."

Carnavon bowed assent, and again motioned to a chair, which the old man declined, but smiled in the declining.

"I heard you speak to-night," he said; then paused. "You were like the picture I have loved to make of young Saul of Tarsus before his feet trod the road to Damascus."

Carnavon was astonished. Not infrequently had he been compelled to listen privately to his opponents, to ministers of the gospel, to zealots who forced themselves upon him to convert or condemn. To all alike, whether they came in humility and

1   5

love, or in heat and with invective on their lips, he had comported himself with the same dignity, the same courtesy, the same self-restraint. But none had been like this little old man in uniform; about none had hovered this spirit of gentle sweetness, of fatherly affection.

"Sir," continued the aged warrior of God's Army of the Streets, "I have not come hoping to convert you to my belief. You are a greater man than I, blessed with greater gifts, and I could not prevail. I have come to ask you one question. Sir, are you sincere? Do you believe in your heart the things you say with your lips?"

"If I did not," replied Carnavon, "I should remain silent."

The old man regarded him steadily,

his expression one almost of affection. "Sir," he said, presently, "can perfect sincerity and one thousand dollars a lecture go hand in hand? When I am gone I ask you to consider this. One, believing in the Master, betrayed Him for thirty pieces of silver; you, not believing in Him, cannot betray Him, but you war on Him with the weapons He gave you—for many times thirty pieces of silver. With your honest unbelief I have no quarrel; when you pass it on to others for gain you do an ill thing. God may forgive the honest doubt—the thirty pieces of silver He cannot forget."

The stranger spoke as to one he loved, without rancor, softening criticism with gentleness. Carnavon was not offended; indeed, he was moved, but waited, making no reply.

7

Again the old man spoke, this time as he retired toward the door.

"Sir, I have liked to think of Saul as I see you. So have I pictured him when he went out in his young strength against the followers of the Master. He traveled his road to Damascus and saw his vision. One day a vision may come to you." He paused in the open door and stretched out his hand with the gesture of one who asks a thrice-valued favor. "If the vision comes, and I am yet alive, will you seek me out? I have not far to go before my race is done, but that would be sweet knowledge for me to carry yonder with me."

Carnavon rose, smiling the smile that drew men to him. "If Saul sees his vision and becomes Paul, he will come to you," he said.

8

Then the door closed on the ancient soldier of peace, and he was gone.

Carnavon having no heaven to look forward to, strove to make his plot of earth more beautiful. His home, a structure to delight the fancy, stood among acres whose loveliness was wrought by art that aided and followed, rather than sought to lead nature. Within the house, wherever the eye rested, were paintings, statues, tapestries, furnishings that made one eager for a longer scrutiny. Vases of exquisite form, antiques from the hands of long-dead masters, medallions wrought by the great Cellini himself, made splendid nook and niche. Indeed, Carnavon loved his medals with a particular affection; they were his avocation, they and their

baser kindred born to commerce —
coins.

No common coin-collector was he;
not for age or rarity or country did
he seek, but for beauty alone. A coin
no bigger than the nail of one's finger,
if it but presented the face of beauty,
gave him greater joy than a canvas
made immortal by Titian or a statue
hewn by the chisel of the demigod
Michael Angelo. In every human
creature is a store of love; love in
desuetude is unthinkable—it must
have an object, worthy or unworthy,
virtuous or depraved. No woman had
nestled into Carnavon's life; religion
he rejected; his medals and coins remained, and he loved them for their
loveliness.

He sat in his library when a servant
entered, saying: "There is a man at

the door who asks to see you. He had no card."

"Ask him his business with me," directed Carnavon.

The man returned presently. "It is about a coin, sir—a rare coin, he says."

"Show him in," said Carnavon.

He arose as the caller entered. The man was of doubtful age; evidently a Hebrew. "Mr. Carnavon?" he asked. Carnavon nodded.

"I have brought for your inspection a rare and, I consider, beautiful coin. I understand you are interested in such."

"Yes," replied Carnavon, "provided they *are* beautiful."

The Hebrew drew a tiny parcel from his pocket, removed a paper wrapping, and disclosed a small metal box. Raising the cover of this, he extracted a small silver coin and extended it to Carnavon.

The master of the house accepted it and moved closer to the light, scrutinizing it jealously. A puzzled expression crossed his face. "I have never seen a similar piece," he said. "Indeed, I must confess I do not identify it. Will you do so for me?"

"It is of Hebrew coinage," explained the dealer. "You will observe in relief the olive branch and the pot of manna. Simon the High Priest had authority to stamp and issue it. Nineteen hundred odd years, you see, is its age, yet it is wonderfully preserved—scarcely worn. I have handled thousands of coins, but none of such antiquity not worn almost to obliteration."

"It is rarely beautiful," admitted Carnavon. "I should like to possess it. What price have you set?"

"Though I am a dealer, I am at a loss to give it a value. Allow me to leave it with you a few days, not as a coin, but as an article of *vertu*. At the end of that time make me an offer."

It was a strange enough proposition, yet fair, and Carnavon acceded instantly. The Hebrew expressed his thanks and took his departure.

Carnavon moved to the inviting depths of a huge chair before the glowing log in the fireplace, and, holding the coin of Simon the High Priest in his palm, leaned forward, the better to possess the beauties of it. Over and over he turned it, marking its perfection of design, the miracle of

2   13

its preservation. A coin of Simon the High Priest! To a master-student of sacred history what scenes were limned at the mention of that name! It was Carnavon's profession to jeer at inconsistencies in the epic of the Passion; to tear it part from part with the scalpel of his remorseless logic; but to deny its poetic beauty must be left to another than he. It was his custom to refer to it as the greatest fiction in the world.

An hour he spent thus, delighting in his new possession. At last, raising his eyes at the sudden darkening of the room, he saw that the room was no longer about him; he was standing in a great court, stone-paved, high-walled, porticoed, and before him rose majestically the pile of a great building, its successive terraces lifting upward and upward in awful grandeur. Carnavon gazed incredulous, for the outline of the structure was familiar to him. He knew that he was standing in the shadow of Solomon's porch, in the court of the Gentiles of Herod's temple in Jerusalem.

As he marveled, a man, furtive of action, appeared from the direction of the gate of Coponius, and strode rapidly inside the confines marked by the *soreg*, beyond which no Gentile dare pass on pain of death. Carnavon knew the law, yet he was drawn to follow, impelled by something outside his own will. Doubtless he would have gone of his own volition, for the man passed so close to him that Carnavon saw his face, the gleaming whites of his eyes; saw terror made more repulsive by cupidity. The cheeks were unnaturally white, their pallor accentuated by the blackness of the hair and beard. One hand was hidden within the folds of the garment, the other was potently expressive; now it closed tightly, trembling with the tension of gripping muscles, now it opened slowly, finger by finger. It was the hand of a man in agony, of a man who suffered torture in soul or body. It was the face that told Carnavon the pain was not physical.

Seeing such a one in such a place alone, Carnavon must have followed.

Within, pacing restlessly up and down in the shadow, was an imposing patriarchal figure, priestly robed, wearing the insignia of the High Priest of Israel. The moonlight fell on his face, and Carnavon read impa-

tience, anxiety, perturbation. Now
and again he lifted his shoulders, ex-
pelled his breath. Toward him the
furtive stranger hastened. Carnavon
stood in the shelter of a pillar and
watched and listened.

The High Priest stopped, bent his
body forward, and scrutinized the
figure that approached him. The
furtive one paused a few paces away,
bent his head obsequiously. His eyes
could not meet the eyes of the High
Priest; perhaps the jewels set in the
priest's breastplate blinded him, for
they gave back the glare of the
moon.

"I have come," said the man. Carnavon could see the trembling of his
hand.

"It is well," said the High Priest,
in guarded tones. As the man drew

17

nearer, the priest drew his garments away as though fearing defilement. "Wilt thou do the thing?"

The man opened his mouth to speak, but words died in his throat; he moved his lower jaw, as one does who talks, but no sound came. He raised his hand, which shook as with a palsy, and wiped his brow. At last he became articulate. "I will do it," he whispered, and shuddered in the speaking.

"The plan and the place, thou knowest them?"

"I know them."

"And the hour?"

"Thy men must watch. . . . The hour I know not. They must watch and follow."

"Where shall they watch?"

"In a place I will show them. . . .

Before going in I will lead them to the spot."

Silence fell. The High Priest frowned darkly, yet his face, strong, crafty, impressive, told of his satisfaction in a desire fulfilled, in an end accomplished. The furtive man stood motionless, an evil thing to look upon.

"By what sign shall my soldiers know Him whom we seek?" asked the High Priest. "Perchance they may mistake another for Him. . . . But thou goest with them to show the way and the place. When thou hast come unto Him, go thou to His side and kiss Him on the cheek as a sign that He is the man and none other." There was scorn in the voice of Simon the High Priest for the instrument that was fitted to his hand.

He turned on his heel and would

have departed, but the furtive man clutched his mantle and detained him. Simon frowned back into that face distorted by avarice, and his eyes grew hard.

"Truly," said he, "I had forgotten thy wage." And forthwith he drew a bag from the folds of his upper garment, and counted money into the hand of the man—and Carnavon counted with him. Thirty times did the fingers of the High Priest enter the bag, and thirty times did a piece of silver drop into the outstretched, trembling claw. The last of the thirty fell from the overflowing palm and rolled to Carnavon's feet, resting in a spot of moonlight. It glittered whitely —and in distinct relief was visible the familiar pot of manna: in every respect it was the fellow of the

ALONG THE ROAD HURRIED AND JOSTLED A THRONG ARMED WITH SWORDS AND STAVES

coin Carnavon still grasped in his hand.

Carnavon looked again, and the temple was not there, neither was the furtive one, nor the High Priest. All about him stretched the darkness, light-dotted; in the distance, toward the city, the mingled voices of approaching tumult affronted the night. Presently along the road hurried and jostled a throng armed with swords and staves, at their head the furtive stranger of the temple, his black beard sunk on his breast. Carnavon was impelled to follow them.

Carnavon outstripped the rabble. The road seemed familiar to him, his destination determined. He hurried onward.

On a hillside he came on a little body of men sleeping. He paused,

3

looked on them, and wondered. Presently, from a little way off came a figure, erect, bare of head, with face majestically sorrowful. Awe of that presence laid itself on Carnavon so that he was fain to avert his eyes. The Man paused by the sleeping group, sighed, shook his head tenderly, and went away again to kneel beside a rock and pray. His voice was audible to Carnavon.

"Oh, my father, if it be possible, let this cup pass from me. . . ."

After a time spent in supplication and anguish of spirit the Man arose, his face lightened, serene, and came again to the sleeping group. Carnavon's eyes filled, for never had he dreamed a face of such gentle bravery. The Man spoke again:

"Sleep on now, and take your rest: behold the hour is at hand. . . ."

While he was speaking the rabble ascended the hill, and at their head cringed the furtive one. The Man watched their approach calmly, but his companions, trembling, gathered about him, pressing close, trembling, calling out in fear.

The furtive one pushed his way to the center of the group, to the very side of the Man, and cried out in a voice hoarse, fearful, quivering, *"Master . . . Master,"* and kissed Him on the cheek. And as he moved, Carnavon could hear the sound of pieces of silver jingling together in his garment.

The Master spoke softly, calmly, with infinite sorrow. *"Judas"*—His eyes rested an instant on the cringing figure—"*betrayest thou the Son of Man with a kiss?*"

Cries of dismay rose weakly from the little group of followers, and they fell away, seeking safety for themselves—all save one, a man of face to remember, who feared, yet was steadfast in defense of Him he loved. This one drew his sword and threw himself before the Master, and as the soldiers of the High Priest pressed forward he smote at them and severed an ear from the head of one of the foremost.

The Master commanded him to put up his weapon, stepped forward a pace, touched the wound with his finger, and it was healed.

Carnavon looked again, and it was daylight in the court of Herod's temple. He passed inward and stood with an assembly about the person of the High Priest Simon, men of weight and dignity, the priests and elders of the people. As he watched them, heads together, discussing some matter of import, there came again the furtive one, now ridden by remorse, by terror, so that his face was ill to look upon, and he approached the High Priest, saying, in a voice like the croaking of a raven, "*I have sinned, . . . I have betrayed the innocent blood,*" and fell upon his knees, his hands full of silver.

The High Priest looked on him coldly, and replied in even tones: "What is that to us? See thou to that."

Whereupon the furtive one flung the silver from him wildly, and rushed out of the temple, Carnavor following, until they came to a lonely place; and there the man hanged himself from a tree so that his feet dangled over a precipice.

Again Carnavon stood by a road-side, and the way was filled with a great multitude, shouting, distracted; in their midst a company of soldiers surrounding the Man who staggered under the weight of a cross—staggered, fell to his knees, for the weight was too great for his strength. The soldiers consulted, then laid hands on a man of the people and made him take up the burden.

The procession moved forward slowly. Behind the man came a company, composed for the most part of women, who wept and raised their voices in sorrow, lamenting His anguish. He turned to them and said, "*Daughters of Jerusalem, weep not for*

me . . ." The remainder of his words
were lost to Carnavon in the general
clamor.

Again, Carnavon stood upon a bare,
forbidding hillside among a shouting, gesticulating throng, and from the
apex of the hill arose three crosses.
Carnavon covered his face, for the
sight was cruel.

From the mob of shouting people
jeers and gibes arose; and one man,
more conspicuous than his fellows,
strode nearer the foot of the central
cross and cried, loudly:

"For thirty pieces of silver was He
sold—this King of the Jews. Doth
not a slave bring more?" And he
continued to utter gibes and rid-
icule.

At last the Man opened His eyes
and regarded His tormentor, not with

anger, not rebukingly, but with majestic calm. It was not a glance to strike terror; it conveyed no anger, no threat; but the tormentor fell silent, awed by its divine loftiness.

It seemed to Carnavon that the Master's eyes sought him out and touched him for an instant, and he sank to the ground, crouching in awe and hiding his face from the eyes of Him he had persecuted.

Suddenly there fell a darkness that was impenetrable. The Master uttered His final words, "*Father, into thy hands I commit my spirit.*" His head sank on His breast; His suffering was done. All about Carnavon reigned confusion, terror. Rumors were rife; men ran hither and yon, not knowing what they did; prodigies were reported from mouth to mouth, and one there was who cried, in a terrible voice, "The curtain of the temple is rent in twain. . . ."

Behold, it was another day. Carnavon stood outside the walls of the Holy City, and the hour was dawn. Along the road which lay before him came two women, one of whom Carnavon recognized as the mother of the Master, and their faces were alight with joy. Carnavon wondered in his heart how this could be. Suddenly there was another figure walking by their side, a Man. Carnavon started, stared in astonishment, for it was a figure that could not be mistaken— the same noble face he had seen in the garden and on the cross. He abased himself, hiding his face. It was the Master whom he had seen crucified, dead, hanging from the cross. It was

3

the Master, risen from the dead, released from His tomb. . . .

Carnavon dared lift his face to look again. The eyes of the Master were fixed on him, met his eyes, and the Master smiled. . . .

Carnavon raised himself to his feet from the depths of his chair before the blazing fire, and passed his hand across his eyes as though to wipe away a film. Then, without movement, he stood staring into the blaze, his face a mask; and so he remained until the log was embers and the blaze a glow. He sighed. His features changed from stoniness to grief, and he raised the hand in which was clasped the piece of silver of the coinage of Simon, opened it, and, bowing his head, gazed reverently on a sacred thing.

Swiftly his bearing altered to determination, to action. He thrust on his coat, his hat, and went out into the night, traversing road and street until he came to the crowded places of the city where men turned night into day. And as he walked he listened. Faintly, borne to his ear on the chill wind, came the sound of singing, of instruments of music, of drums, and he smiled.

In a public square huddled a shivering, squalid crowd, its nucleus a little band of uniformed soldiers of the Cross—men and women. As Carnavon approached, the music ceased; a small, tottering old man, silvery of hair and beard, doffed his cap and stepped to the center of the circle, raising his hand for silence. Carnavon had found whom he sought; it was the stranger of the hotel room.

Carnavon made his way through the fringe of idle listeners, swayed to the side of the praying old man, and, urged to impatience by emotion, waited not for him to cease. He clutched an extended hand, and, broken-voiced, cried: "*I have sinned. . . . I have betrayed the innocent blood!*"

The old preacher of the streets paused, looked on Carnavon's face, and over his wrinkled features spread a look of perfect peace, of richest happiness.

"You—you have stood on the road to Damascus—" he whispered, hands groping for Carnavon's hands.

"And I have seen a vision," Carnavon said, simply.

THE END

The Sale of an Appetite

STILL HE STOOD THERE, GLUED TO THE SPOT, FEASTING HIS
EYES AND AGGRAVATING THE HUNGER OF HIS BELLY.

The Sale of an Appetite

By PAUL LAFARGUE

Translated by Charles H. Kerr
Illustrated by Dorothy D. Deene

CHICAGO
Charles H. Kerr & Company
1904

PREFACE

Some years ago an attendant in the insane asylum at Charenton gave me a manuscript which had been entrusted to him by one of the inmates, who had died in a strait-jacket. Its author, Emile Destouches, the attendant asserted, had never been insane; he had without doubt been committed by the orders of some high official; for, during his captivity, they kept him alone, watched by a special guard, who came from outside.

The three hundred sheets, which the attendant gave me and which I still have, are penciled with a feverish hand, evidently written in haste, in a dimly lighted cell. They contain the story which follows. It seemed to me so strange that till now I have hesitated to publish it. But recent studies of specialists on hypnotism and cerebral dualism have revealed such curious phenomena that all current ideas on consciousness, free will, and even human individuality are thrown into confusion. I think, then, that I shall do a service to physiological science by printing the story of Emile Destouches. I need only mention similar cases reported by Chamisso, Mary Shelley, Hoffman, Balzac and recently Besant and Rice. Physicians should collate and compare these extraordinary facts, stated by trustworthy men, study them, and discover their relations to the miracles of religion, which they rob of their supernatural character.

I have been obliged to decipher, disentangle and harmonize the manuscript, but so far as possible I have respected the form given it by the prisoner—the reader will judge whether I should say the madman—of Charenton. I have put his narrative into the third person, and have suppressed certain pathological descriptions which might prove too realistic for the taste of readers outside the medical profession.   P. L.

Part I

PART I.

It was in the month of December. It was cold, and Emile Destouches was terribly hungry. The snow whitened the pavements, an icy wind pierced the thickest cloaks and forced the scattered pedestrians to hasten their steps. His face blue, his teeth chattering, and his limbs shivering, Emile stood where he had planted himself before the show-window of a restaurant, brilliantly lighted. A five-foot sturgeon reclined in majesty upon a bed of greens; white and plump pullets, their legs in the air, were innocently exposing their hinder parts; larks, plovers and ortolans were encased in slices of bacon; shining apples and magnificent pears, en-

veloped in lace paper, were reclining lux-
uriously in the padding of the hampers.
A gigantic pie, flanked with silvery sau-
sages and spotted mortadelles, absorbed
his entire attention; the pie was ripped
open so as to expose its rosy flesh, veined
with fat livers and marbled with truffles.
Emile opened wide his gluttonous eyes,
and clinched his thirty-two long and
sharp teeth.

For three days the unhappy man had
eaten nothing, extreme hunger twisted and
lacerated his intestines, contracted the
muscles of his jaws and filled his mouth
with saliva. There he was, motionless,
not feeling the cold, petrified at the sight
of that divine substance which might ap-
pease his hunger, end his sufferings and
fill his whole being with earthly delights.

A fragile window-pane separated him from the object of his desires. One blow of his fist would have broken the window and put the coveted pie within his grasp; indeed he need only have turned the knob of the door, pushed it, stretched out his arm, to have seized and carried to his mouth the joy of his stomach. Still he stood there, glued to the spot, feasting his eyes and aggravating the hunger of his belly. The coward! The man in a state of nature, the savage, would have eaten, and simply said, I am hungry! But the fear of the policeman, and the dread of the moral indignation of our civilized mobs against every flagrant misdemeanor broke his arms and his legs, paralyzing and stifling the imperious cries of nature. And yet what had the wretched fellow to fear? He was dying of hunger, and to end his torture he was thinking of suicide.

"What use to live!—I might find something to eat this evening; but what should I have to fight away hunger tomorrow, the next day, all the days? Why struggle to live when every reason for living is lost, when life is nothing but misery? Enough of it! Miserable starveling, feast your eyes on your last banquet!"

In his feverish passion, he was talking aloud.

A gentleman of near fifty years, tall and extremely fat, with black beard and hair, a bloated face and an enormous abdomen confined with difficulty in a vast overcoat buttoned with much trouble, observed him attentively. He placed his hand on Emile's shoulder.

"You wish to kill yourself?"

"Yes," he answered mechanically.

"You wish to kill yourself because you are hungry?"

"Yes."

"You are young, well built, you are the man I am looking for; follow me."

Emile believed in a providential savior; he obeyed with alacrity. The unknown entered Vefour's, went up the steps to the parlor floor, settled himself in a private compartment and with a friendly gesture invited the young man to seat himself. A little bread was on the table, the starving man bit into it ravenously.

"A little patience, my friend, be careful

of your appetite, that most precious of blessings; wait for the chicken soup."

In a twinkling Emile emptied the plate of soup; the oysters arrived.

"You are murdering yourself, why, it is a shame to eat bread with your oysters; taste them by themselves!"

The fat man took nothing; lost in admiration, he watched, supervised and counseled his guest.

"Be moderate. Do not come back to that quail entree—save yourself for the roast fowl—remember that the lobster salad is still to come."

Just as a skilful jockey restrains the ardor of his thoroughbred, he tempered the voracity of the young man; he desired by judicious halts and scientific delays to prolong his happiness and make him taste its moments more slowly. Emile made several attempts to thank his singular benefactor.

"Do not distract your appetite by talking; you will not often have it in such good condition; I would give a thousand francs, ten thousand francs, for an appetite as capacious as yours. Eating is the supreme duty. All religions make of it a sacred rite, the most solemn ceremony of Catholicism is the communion, the mastication of God, the theophagic Eucharist. Eating should always be in a religious silence, that the thought may be entirely concentrated on the act that is being performed. The monks, those sublime masters of the gastronomic art, imposed silence in the refectory."

"Ouf! I can eat no more!—I owe you many thanks."

"Keep them for a better occasion; as I am neither a philanthropic free-thinker nor a charitable Christian, I have nothing to do with your gratitude. You have appeased your belly and regained your ears, now listen to me. When you were gazing at the window display of the restaurant with looks burning enough to melt the fat on the hams, I said to myself with envy, if I only possessed such an appetite! Gold, of which I have more than a Jew, procures pleasures of the intelligence and the senses, but I despise them; appetite is above intelligence, above love. I live only by the belly and for the belly, I enjoy only when I eat or when I drink; the rest is vanity. I am Sch————, that will inform you that my fortune is stupendous; I do not know the number of my millions; at the age of thirty-two I was a coal and railroad king. I can intoxicate myself with the kisses of love and the fumes of ambition, I can gather all the joys of earth, but I despise them all, all, understand. I would give all the pleasures that men pursue for one of the dinners of my chief cook, the ingenious and scientific chemist, the only man whom I love and esteem. If Solomon, whom Jehovah touched with his wisdom, grew weary of men and of God and satiated with the realities of life and the dreams of his intellect until he exclaimed, "All is vanity," it is because he had only exhausted the pleasures of love, the joys of reason and the satisfaction of absolute rule, while he was ignorant of the supreme delights of the table. What is love? A miserable and fleeting pleasure; it has scarcely begun, when snap!—it is shattered, vanished—ended. Compared with this, the joys of the stomach seem eternal; they last delicious hours. The common herd have been wiser than Solomon; all nations, the African negro as well as the yellow man of China, have taken as visible sign of social superiority the expanded belly, the belly enormous and round like the globe. The capitalist bourgeoisie, the class which rules the world, the class of which I am one of the high and mighty representatives, has disemburdened itself of all intellectual and manual labor to devote itself to the exclusive development of the belly, to create the race of the Ventripotents. Do you know what is the most remarkable fact of this century-end, the fact which best characterizes our epoch? It is neither the discovery of the telephone, nor the invention of dynamite, nor the insurrection of the Commune, nor the defeat of Sedan; it is that little medal struck by order of the artists, the men of letters, the journalists, the philosophers, the scientists, the fine flower of the intellectual and refined bourgeoisie, to remind the coming centuries that within Paris all besieged, bombarded, blood-sprinkled, pulsing with battle-fever and crying with hunger, they, as usual, ate well and drank well; what sublime magnanimity of soul must have been theirs to rise thus above the miseries and pains which surround them, that

they might fulfill with serenity and free-
dom of spirit the first and most important of human functions.*

"The Hindus, those masters of abstract
metaphysics, arrive at the most mystical
ecstacy through contemplating the navel,
the central point of the human belly. The
belly is the true God of humanity; it is
for its satisfaction alone that men plow
the earth and sail the seas. The belly is

---

*The medal referred to by Sch—— (Des-
touches never spells his name out) was struck
at the Paris mint, in honor of the restaurant-
keeper, Paul Brebant. On its face it reads:

During the siege of Paris, certain persons, accustomed to meet every fortnight with M.
Brebant, never once observed that they were dining in a besieged city of two million souls.
1870-71.

The reverse of the medal read as follows:

TO MONSIEUR PAUL BREBANT.

Ernest Renan, Paul de St-Victor, M. Berthelot,
Ch. Blanc, Scherer, Dumesnil, A. Nefftzer, Ch.
Edmond, Thurot, Marey, E. de Goncourt, J. Bert-
rand, Theophile Gautier, A. Hebrard.

the spring of human actions always stretched and never broken, it is to gorge it that men transport and bring together in great capitals the products of all climes; its needs and its appetites, numerous, voracious and ever renewed, unite in brotherhood the peoples of the universe. Devil take me, I believe I am making a speech. This subject always lifts me into the ideal. Let us return to earth. Ah! what a sorry animal is man! How imperfect, how inferior to the other beasts of the earth; nature has behaved toward him like a stepmother; she has neither given him the interminable gullet of the giraffe, to taste long and slowly the fragrance of wines, nor the hot and insatiable stomach of the duck, to digest always without wearying; she has treated this pretended king of creation more harshly than the intestinal worms, the toenias, those thrice-happy beings which bathe themselves in their nourishing fluid, drinking it in through all their pores and always! Man's stomach is limited, wretchedly limited, and to cap the climax of our miseries, we have eyes larger than our belly. But if my stomach shares the weaknesses of humanity, I can at least extend and reinforce its power by buying the appetite of another, just as my brother capitalists buy the virtue and the conscience of their fellow men. I propose, then, that you sell me your digestive power, as my laborers sell me their muscular powers, my engineers their intellectual powers, my cashiers their honesty and the nurses who care for my children their milk and their maternal cares."

"Is it possible?"

"Perfectly so. You produce and furnish the appetite, I will eat and drink for you and you will be satisfied. The moralists, who are untoward and melancholy bipeds, teach solemnly the contempt of what they call disdainfully the pleasures of the flesh; you are young and simple enough to indulge such scruples. Sell me your appetite, which condemns you to labor and poverty, and you shall have money to pay for the pleasures of which you are now deprived. I will allow you a monthly income of 1,500 francs."

"But—"

"No buts! you don't think that enough? Call it two thousand. Consider that if you reject my offer, you will not know where to sleep this evening or where to get your breakfast tomorrow, and if you agree to the bargain the pretty girls of the boulevard will welcome you to their beds."

Emile's eyes sparkled.

"Two thousand francs! two thousand francs a month, that suits me. What must I do?"

"Sign a contract before a notary. Don't look at me that way; I am not Satan, what the devil!—I am just an ordinary mortal, like you. But no living being possesses my power; my science surpasses that of other men. Not all the power of Napoleon I. nor all the science of Darwin gave them the ability to dine twice a day; I possess this mysterious and precious faculty. The nineteenth century, as was declared by the great philosopher of the bourgeoisie, Auguste Comte, is the century of altruism; never, in fact, at any other epoch, has there been such a complete understanding of how to make use of other people. The exploitation of man by the capitalist is so perfected that the most personal qualities, those most inherent in the individual, have been utilized to the profit of another. For the defense of his property the capitalist no longer depends on his own courage, but upon that of certain proletarians disguised as soldiers; the banker consumes the honesty of his cashier, and the manufacturer the vital force of his workmen, as the debauchees use the sex-nature of the Venuses of the pavement. Nevertheless two faculties have as yet escaped our capitalist altruism, the child-bearing faculty of woman and the digestive faculty; no one has yet been able to transform them into goods that can be bought and sold, as are already the innocence of the virgin, the sanctity of the priest, the conscience of the legislator, the brilliancy of the writer and the intelligence of the chemist. The man who shall work that miracle will be greater than Charlemagne and wiser than Newton; he will be the most beneficent of the benefactors of the poor. Then the rich woman will no longer deform her figure by carrying in her abdomen, through long and painful months, the fruit of her womb; she will deposit her fertilized ovum in the womb of a poor woman, and during the nine months that the one who has sold her womb shall be fattening with the blood of her flesh the fetus of the capitalist's wife, she will have a respite from her poverty; for the first time she will rest herself, eating and drinking to her heart's content. The poor man will no longer have to dread his terrible enemy, hunger; he will cultivate his appetite, which will be the merchandise sought by the millionaire, always in quest of that sovereign good, which Greek philosophy never could discover. What a resource the poor will then have—as for me, I know the useful art of having what I eat digested by another; I shall not reveal that secret until on my death-bed."

"You are joking."

"No, my friend, to have digested by another the meats that my stomach takes is in the last analysis neither more wonderful nor more incomprehensible than to have executed at London or at New York, thanks to the telegraph, the thought that my brain conceives, and at the instant it conceives it. I am so far from joking that here are two thousand francs for the first month.

Sch——— and Destouches proceeded to the office of M. Gabarit, who drew up a paper, scrupulously worded, which the two contracting parties signed and sealed. Emile Destouches sold for five years his appetite in consideration of two thousand francs a month, which Sch——— was to pay him in advance. When the contract was signed, Emile took a drink which plunged him into a deep slumber. He awoke to find himself at a restaurant table sitting in front of two beer schooners and a plump girl who was laughing foolishly that she might show her pretty teeth. He thought he was dreaming; he felt of himself, pinched himself; he rattled in his pocket the pieces of gold he had just received; he was no longer hungry; it had really happened. Only the devil knows where he finished the evening so strangely begun.

Part II

BETWEEN TIMES HE CAUGHT ON THE WING THE PLEASURES
OF WHICH POVERTY HAD DEPRIVED HIM.

PART II.

All that is new is beautiful, says the wisdom of the nations. The beginnings of his new existence delighted Emile Destouches; at ten each morning, like a believer visited by the supernatural, he felt descend into his stomach meats and drinks which he neither ate nor drank; he did not perceive their odor nor their flavor, but he was obliged to digest them; his stomach was filled by an operation as mystical as that which fertilized the virgin Mary and gave Joseph a little Jesus.

The repasts which he took through the mouth and gullet of his master who had leased him lasted two hours; with his head heavy and his limbs languid, he

slept a part of the day, digesting slowly
and painfully the meats and the wines
which the other had greedily swallowed.
Toward three o'clock he went out for a
long walk to revive his gorged belly; this
was required of him by one of the clauses
of the contract. In the evening his stomach was again filled, and he sank into an
ophidian sleep. These heroic repasts were
not repugnant to his vigorous peasant's
constitution, and between times he caught
on the wing the pleasures of which poverty had deprived him; he dressed ele-
gantly and ran around with the girls.

"I am nothing any more but a grub-
sack," he said to himself, "my life is the
life of the geese that are crammed for
their fat livers; I do not taste the wines
nor the meats which I am compelled to

digest for my employer. Bah! the people
who have lost their sense of smell are in
the same case with me; and then, it will
last only five years; during that time of
forced labor of the stomach, not only
shall I be relieved from the labor of mastication and the degrading concern for
bread to be found day by day, but I shall
save ten or even twenty thousand francs
a year. The laborers who are condemned
all their lives to the forced labors of the
mine and the work-shop would envy my
lot."

Thus he tried to console himself by
comparing his labor to that of other wage
workers; he said to himself that his servitude was temporary and that when it
should be ended, he would have amassed

a pretty sum which would enable him to live like a bourgeois, doing nothing.

The open air exercise and the labors of Venus to which he devoted himself did not prevent this systematic stuffing from reacting on his robust health; he grew dyspeptic; his stomach became sluggish, his disposition melancholy. M. Gabarit. at whose office he drew his monthly salary, reproved him sharply, reproaching him for his festive nights in the company of gay girls; venereal excesses, the notary insisted, blunted his appetite er, which, having been sold, no longer and weakened his digestive power, belonged to him; he should consider him- which, having been sold, no longer belonged to him; he should consider him- self in the position of a farm hand, hired by the year, not allowed to dispose of either his time or his strength at his own fancy, but compelled to regulate them according to the needs of the one who hired him. Emile then thought of marriage and of country life.

"I will hunt, ride horseback, plow my fields; my stomach will regain its former vigor and will endure without weariness the loads imposed upon it by my employer."

He reduced his love passages and redoubled his exercises at the gymnasium; but in proportion as he fortified his stomach and increased its digestive capacity, his employer increased the quantity of victuals which he engulfed.

The notary found a young lady to marry, agreeable in appearance, of a respectable family and with a round dowry. The conditions of the marriage contract having been discussed and fixed, the time came for the official introduction of the betrothed pair to each other. Emile, barbered, brushed and burnished, arrived, radiant with hope; he saw himself a landed proprietor, supervising the cultivation of his fields and the care of his live stock. It was three o'clock when his employer had put into his stomach the last mouthful of his ogre-like breakfast, and according to his custom he should have left his wage-worker time to digest it. But scarcely had Destouches entered the parlor of his future mother-in-law, when he felt his stomach, still overloaded, filling itself anew. His employer had just experienced certain annoyances and was in a murderous temper; to dispel his trouble he sat down at the table and began to eat and drink with fury; the mouthfuls and the bumpers that he engulfed were enormous, and succeeded each other without respite. Poor Emile could do no more; the walls of his stomach were distended to bursting; he sank into an easy chair, exuding at every pore an icy and fetid sweat; nausea overpowered him; he could not resist. Summoning his last strength, he dashed out of the parlor, and on the staircase, he relieved himself of the solids and liquids which his employer had gulped down. But in proportion as he emptied his stomach, his monster, like the task-master of the Danaids, continued to fill it. He spread filth and bad odors through the house—in his shame, he dragged himself into the street and gave up his projects of marrying.

Another day the employer was eating almonds and drinking a heavy Spanish wine; Destouches was digesting at the hippodrome of Longchamps, while he watched the horses running; all of a sudden he loses his head, jostles the men, tears the women's dresses and slaps a policeman; he is packed off to the station house to sleep off the wine that his employer had drunk. The next day he is taken before the judge. "If only my drunken master doesn't begin his libations again!" he murmured.

The thing he feared came to pass. The fumes of the wine which ascended from his stomach intoxicated him anew; he insulted the court in full session, he achieved a sentence of two years in prison, for insults to the magistracy, but three days later his all-powerful master secured his release.

The gastric labor of Destouches became every day more difficult and more painful; the ogre repeated his repasts four and five times in the twenty-four hours, and many times a day drank to the point of intoxication. Emile resorted for consolation to the practice of the Romans, he took an emetic, but every time he emptied his stomach, his torturer filled it up again. His life was intolerable. The sight of any food, even bread, gave him nausea. The disgust which the satiated and impotent feel for the multitude and for everything that lives, cries and moves entered into his soul; he fled from the society of men and the sight of their habitations; he lived alone, in the midst of the fields, going out only at night so as not to meet any living being, man or beast; and night and day he labored to digest the heroic banquets of his employer. The fear of poverty, that faithful companion of his youth, had prevented him from breaking his contract, but he owned himself vanquished, and would gladly have chosen days without bread, rather than this terrible labor, this stomach always digesting. He betook himself to M. Gabarit, determined to break the contract; the notary declared up and down that it was impossible; he was bound for three years more, and even if it killed him, he must go on to the end. By way of consolation he added:

"You complain because you have been

reduced to becoming nothing but a digest-ive apparatus; but all who earn their living by working are lodged at the same sign. They obtain their means of existence only by confining themselves to being nothing but an organ functioning to the profit of another; the mechanic is the arm which forges, taps, hammers, planes, digs, weaves; the singer is the larynx which vocalizes, warbles, spins out notes; the engineer is the brain which calculates, which arranges plans; the prostitute is the sexual organ which gives out venereal pleasure. Do you imagine that the clerks in my office use their intelligence, or that they reflect when they are copying papers? Oh, but they don't; thinking is not their business; they are nothing but fingers which scribble. They perform in my offices for ten or twelve hours this work which is far from exhilarating, which gives them headaches, stomach disorders and hemorrhoids; and at evening they carry home writing to finish, that they may earn a few cents to pay their landlord. Console yourself, my dear sir, these young people suffer as well as you, and not one of them has the satisfaction of saying that he receives per year the sum that you draw for a single month of digestive labor."

"It is sad, terribly sad, and I have not even the consolation of believing myself the most unhappy of mortals."

"Imprint this truth on your memory; the poor man no longer exists for himself in our civilized societies, but for the capitalist, who sets him to work at his fancy

or according to his needs with such or
such of his organs."

Emile Destouches went out from the
office broken-hearted. He wandered
through the streets as at that former time
when hunger tortured his entrails. Never
had he felt so miserable; the present was
without joys and the future without
hopes. He observed with despair the
rapid exhaustion of his vitality, he was
emaciated till he had no more than the
skin on his bones; the food which he digested did not nourish him, it only tra-
versed his body, leaving behind it a dull
sense of hunger, and headaches which
made him almost crazy.

While he, with death in his soul, was
wandering aimlessly around, his employer, his joyful employer, was eating

and drinking, and causing masses of food heavy as lead to fall into his stomach.

"Ah! What miseries! My body racked with pain, disgusted with everything would stop to suffer in peace, but this executioner to whom I have sold more than my soul, imposes upon me labor unceasing. In death alone I shall find repose."

Mad with pain and tired of life, he walked along the wharves; the water attracted him, he threw himself into the river. He was fished out and taken home, calmed by his cold bath.

The next day a solidly built fellow brought him a letter from Sch——; it announced to him that from that time to the expiration of his contract of servitude, he would live under the surveillance of the bearer of the letter.

"My little fellow," said his keeper brutally, I am your overseer; no more farces, understand! You no longer belong to yourself, you have sold your appetite and roped in forty-eight thousand plunks, now you have to live and you have no right to kill yourself. If you were to take your life what would become of our employer? The dear man, doesn't he need to digest what he eats? There's no other way. His belly must rest, so yours must work. I give you warning that the first time you try suicide again, I will box you up like a lunatic, those are my orders. But don't worry, you will not grow old at it, I have watched two others before you, and they died at a gallop. What an ogre our capitalist is, by thunder! His appetite comes as he eats, it's all very fine for him; he isn't the one who gets the indigestions. He crams until the digesting machine that he has bought bursts."

"To die of indigestion! That is my future."

A new life began. Like the artisans who work at home for their employer, Emile had up to that time lived with a shadow of liberty, but from that day, like the proletarian imprisoned in his employer's factory, he was to digest under the eye of an overseer. Overwhelmed by the monumental repasts of his employer, he had suspended his hygienic walks, prescribed by the contract; he passed his days and nights, extended at full length, moving only to perform the most necessary physiological functions. But his keeper was commissioned to see to the rigorous execution of the contract that had been drawn up; not a moment of the precious time he had sold was to be wasted. At the break of day he dragged him from his bed and obliged him to take long walks in the fields in order to prepare a morning appetite for the employer. In the afternoon, when filled up to the neck and stretched out on his back, he would have wished to remain motionless, but he was obliged to put himself on the march, in order to promote the current process of digestion and to prepare for his employer a new appetite, fresh and solid.

Emile had his caprices of revolt.

"Don't kick, my little fellow." said his

overseer at the first sign of insubordination, "you are dealing with too strong a party, you will get hurt. I have in my portfolio the doctor's certificates, the orders from police headquarters, the judge's permission, in fact the whole business for chucking you into Charenton! And there I will take you with a club, like the convicts."

Emile, cast down, stupified, dejected, lived without will power, always digesting, always ill, always trembling, he lay down, rose, walked, stopped, sat at the command of the overseer, submissive and mute like a whipped poodle-dog that dares not bark.

One morning the employer had devoured a breakfast more formidable than usual; he had gobbled down tureenfuls of

fish soup and had gorged himself on
dishes of cod, kilogrammes of meat and
mountains of macaroni. Emile was
crushed, he slept heavily for two hours;
when his overseer put him on his feet for
the regulation walk, this enormous mass
of undigested food bore down like a dead
weight on his stomach. He went along
heavily by the side of his guard, dragging
his legs painfully, with his head sadly inclined forward; at a turn of the road he
dashed into a group of men and women
talking and laughing. Sch——— was
strutting along in the center, the gayest
of all, his coarse and noisy laugh sounded
like a flourish of trumpets, while his fellow revelers were ready to faint from lis-
tening.

"What boorish gaiety," said one of

them, "would any one believe that this animal has just been murdering himself with victuals that would have been too much for ten peasants who had gone hungry for three days?"

The sight of his employer happy and in good humor inspired Destouches with a resolution, he pressed through the crowd and threw himself at his feet. He wept, related his griefs, his disgust, implored pity, begged that he be delivered from his abominable slavery, offered to return the money that he had received; he asked only one favor, to be allowed to rest, and no longer digest for another.

"What does that lunatic want?" said Sch———, repulsing him with his foot.

The guard seized Emile by the collar, raised him from the earth and dragged

"What Does that Lunatic Want?"

him across several fields. Once at their lodgings, he belabored him with blows.

"That will teach you to trouble the digestion of our employer."

Destouches submitted passively, like a dejected steer; but sometimes even cattle become enraged.

"I have labored, I have suffered that the other might enjoy, I have endured everything; at the end of my strength I have wept, I have implored, and I have been beaten. Death is near at hand. Come! take courage, there is nothing to lose."

Escaping from the custody of the overseer, after getting him intoxicated, he runs to the house of his torturer. Sch———, jocose and rubicund. his body active and his mind cheerful, was about to seat himself at the table. Terror seized him at seeing Emile Destouches, disheveled, haggard, a pistol tightly grasped in his hand.

"Help!—don't kill me!"

"You coward, you villain, you hog, you glutton! You have tortured me, you have put others to a painful death and you would like to kill more still,—you have done your last eating!

With a revolver shot full in his belly, he stretched him on the earth. Thinking him dead, he went to the police office and told his story; the commissioner thought him crazy; his overseer arrived out of breath, and confirmed him in that opinion, which the medical specialists corroborated learnedly. Sch———, cured of his wound, resumed after a few weeks the course of his exaggerated repasts. Emile Destouches was shut up in Charenton and treated to a course of shower-bath and strait-jacket, for having sold his appetite.

THE END.

THE CEDAR BOX

'For thee, mother,' he said. 'And I made
it all with my own hands—all for thee.'

THE
CEDAR BOX

BY
JOHN OXENHAM

*With Frontispiece
from a Drawing by T. Baines*

THIRD IMPRESSION

LONGMANS, GREEN AND CO.
55 FIFTH AVENUE, NEW YORK
39 PATERNOSTER ROW, LONDON
TORONTO, BOMBAY, CALCUTTA, AND MADRAS
1926

To
MY WIFE
IN LOVING ESTIMATION

THE CEDAR BOX

I HAVE had a very strange experience, and as is frequently the case with the highest and most unique of one's experiences, I cannot explain it. All I can do is to tell you the facts as simply as possible and leave you to form your own opinion.

My own is settled unalterably, but then I had the advantage of seeing with my own eyes that which I can only do my best to make you see through this poor and imperfect medium of words.

If only you had seen for yourselves. . . .

I suppose to most of us who live by the pen there is always—locked tight out of sight in that dark little chamber of the heart of which we alone hold the key—the dreadful lurking fear that the time may come when the fecund brain will cease to yield, when the power of creation—glorious even on the limited scale which has been vouchsafed to us—shall fail, and we shall become—what?

As other men? That is hardly possible. This one golden strand, entrusted to us by the Master of our Craft, we have spun with heart and brain and with infinite joy. We have given our lives to it and the best that was in us.

Can we then at the fatal word pick up the dull gray threads of life and of them weave us garments for our nakedness and a trifle for a crust?

Hardly possible. We have lived on the slopes and the hill-tops and watched the strife and turmoil all about us. We have, maybe, done our best to help and hearten, even if only by amusing, the busy ones below. But we have been out of the fight that never ceases in the plains, and how shall we now descend into it and find room to strive and live?

Do not mistake me. It is not that, under such condition of dire necessity, we would not, but simply that we hardly could.

Wise, or otherwise, we may be in our own little conceits, but our wisdom, or our folly, has turned our feet away from the market-place and set them in the by-paths of the hill-sides. We

8

have viewed it all from the outside and turned to our own uses the reek and the clamour and the peculiar ways of it. Some of us have now and again dug out a diamond and done our best with it, and some have been content to dabble in the mud and make thereof unwholesome pies and evil stenches.

But the trouble of it is that we have, of intention and of necessity, held ourselves more or less aloof from the actual world-strife. Our hands have grown unaccustomed to the ever-changing weapons of warfare. The places are all filled, and eager crowds of specially-trained supers are waiting anxiously to leap into the first gaps in the ranks that offer. A man falls, a thousand volunteers rush for his post at half his pay, and the grim fight for life goes on.

I had been ill, literally, in the good old phrase, sick unto death.

After a sudden break and a quick descent I had, for one long day, lain there looking Death full in the face. And I had found it a very tender and gentle face, with friendly, welcoming eyes.

9

For myself, death has never held the terrors some folks feel, for I have always believed that the change when it comes will be for the infinitely better—for the infinitely best.

For myself, then, I had no fears. But for those I must leave behind me, and leave so inadequately provided for,—for my wife and the children, my heart was sick and sore.

It would make such a difference,—all the difference between enough and less than enough. And in that, perhaps, lies the bitterness of death for most of us. For those endowed with a superfluity of this world's goods the bitterness lies— one is given to understand—in the fact that they must leave it all behind them when they go. After all, it is better to regret people than things.

Life had been somewhat of a struggle, you see. Even the by-paths and hill-sides are crowded in these days. Still the fight had been to my liking and I had enjoyed it to the full.

I had nothing to blame myself with, unless with overworking, and that may perchance be reckoned half a virtue. But it was hard to be stricken down like this, just when, at long last, the tide seemed about to turn my way ; and it was bitter beyond words to lie there unable to lift a finger to better matters.

Friend Death shook me gently by the hand that day, and then, to the visible surprise of my good old Doctor Rothie and my tenderest of nurses, with a gracious nod and a smiling 'au revoir,' he went softly away and, against all the accepted canons of the profession, I slept quietly back into life.

But apparently—and to myself without a doubt—to but a broken life which, as it seemed to me, would be worse than none.

My mind, so far as the creative faculty was concerned, was an absolute blank—a dull, vacuous darkness without a living creature in it. I did not believe I would ever write another line of my own.

And I lay and wondered dully what would be the end of it all for all of us.

What could I possibly turn my hand to ? What on earth could I do that should earn even the meagrest living for those dependent on me ?

One has heard of quondam race-horses degraded to the shafts of the sprightly hansom.

I hope it is not true. They would be so very much better dead,—they have no one dependent on their earnings.

And one hears still ghastlier tales of men of birth and education carrying sandwich-boards in the gutter. True, the chances are that, if it is so, the fault is their own, and as a rule it caught them by the throat out of a glass. None the less horrible to think of, however it came about.

At first I was, I suppose, too weak to think very deeply even of the future. But as I grew stronger the grim thought of it grew stronger too and left no room for any thought besides.

Stories ? Books ? Had I written stories and books ? I ? How on earth had I managed it ? I ? With a brain like this—dull as a ditch, empty as a drum, and a heart as heavy as lead.

And this baleful brooding did not make for health. My heart was sick, my eye was clouded with the shadow of the evil days to come, my whole body was full of darkness.

What could I possibly find to do, now that my chosen work was over ? What would become of them all ?

For myself, better, oh, infinitely better, if old Friend Death had gripped me tight that day and refused to let me go. But, for them . . .

This went on for a fortnight or so, the torment of it growing ever greater, and Rothie's kind old face pinched despairingly over me in spite of himself.

He knew all about me, and pretty well all my circumstances, and he was wise enough, and experienced enough, to fathom my depths.

He talked to me cheerfully, rallied me cheerily, told me strange stories of his own experiences, prophesied great things for the future. Did all he could. But I *knew*. My writing days were over, and what was to be the complexion of the days to come was beyond me, except that it was black.

'Ye mustna look like that, laddie,' said Rothie, moved one day to strong expostulation. 'Ye've done splendidly and I'm prood o' ye. Ye're a feather in ma cap, my man.'

'Just that!' I growled; 'a feather—especially about the head, and as fushionless and useless.'

'Ye're weak yet. It'll be all right when ye pick up a bit. Ye're alive anyway, and that's

13

more than ye've any right to be, seeing the state you were in.'

' Ay, I sometimes wish ——'

' No, you don't. I know better. You're not built that way. Take my word for it, my boy. It'll all come back as soon as ye tone up—and with added experience and greater power.'

But my head wagged dolefully to the tune of my heart. ' I know better, Doctor. I'm done. It's only what I'm going to do that troubles me.'

' Do, man ? Why—write—as ye never wrote before. What else would ye do ? That's what ye were made for.'

' That's just it. What else can I do ? I've been asking myself that over and over again till I'm sick of it. And the answer is always— nothing—unless it's sandwich-boards or a hansom-cab.'

' Sandwich fiddlesticks ! Hansoms be hanged !' —it was a stronger word he used. He could be very brusque at times. ' It's sheer nonsense and blithering havers ye're talking. And it is na good for ye to lie brooding over things like that.'

' Old hen on a china egg ! And nothing comes of it.'

14

'It will, ma broodie-hen,' he said, with that somewhat rare smile of his. 'There's mair cheek'ns to be hatched yet than the world kens o', and bonnier birds too.'

It is only to his best-known that he develops the breadth of his native tongue. To the rest his language is most pedantically precise. Rothie talking braid Scots is the very best friend a man can have, especially if he is a sick man.

'Ye shall dedicate your next book to me,' he said, 'and it's a prood man I'll be, for it'll be a thumper.'

'You'll die a humble man, Doctor.'

'We'll see. I'm no a betting-man, but I'm prepared to stake my bill on that dedication.'

'It's brain I'm short of, man, not conscience. Why should I rook you?' At which he only laughed.

The following day when he came in he brought with him a parcel—it seems strange to me now to write of it so—an oblong parcel done up in brown paper and actually tied with string!

It looked like books—or it might have been an electric battery, or a camera, or a set of jig-saw puzzles, or any similar toy suitable to the capacity of a worn-out brain.

He looked at me with a curious smile on his face.

' I'm going to lend you this for a day or two,' he said, with a strangely soft inflection of the voice.

' What is it?' I asked listlessly.

' I'll show you.'

He untied the string as carefully and cautiously as though the contents were frailest glass, opened the brown paper, and discovered an inner wrapping of dark blue velvet. This he unfolded with the same delicate care, and disclosed a metal box about a foot long and nine inches wide.

It was, I judged, of Eastern make. In colour it was of a very rich dark blue, so wonderful in its strange depths as to seem almost semi-transparent. The whole surface was damascened with faint gold tracery of most chaste and exquisite design.

' What lovely workmanship!' exclaimed my wife, who was watching anxiously. She had enormous faith in Rothie, simply because she hails from Renfrewshire, and he from Dumbarton.

' Yes,' he said, with that same soft inflection of

the voice which was so very different from his usual hearty bluffness.

'Jewels?' I asked accommodatingly. If his object was to arouse my interest and lift my thoughts for a moment above my china egg he undoubtedly succeeded. But it was more by the strangeness of his own manner than by his treasure-box.

'We shall see,' was the enigmatic answer to my question.

'What's it made of?'

'I'll tell you all about it later.'

'It is very beautiful,' said my wife, running a slender finger along the interwoven coils of the design and peering into the dark blue depths. 'I feel as if I could see into it, but I can't. It looks miles deep. It is like a great blue-black opal or a mountain tarn.'

'Anything inside?' I asked, to please him with a show of interest.

He drew out his old leather purse, took from it a small wash-leather bag, and out of it a tiny key, steel-blue and gold like the rest. He unlocked the box and quietly raised the lid, and we bent over eagerly to see the contents.

The box was empty. There was nothing to

be seen but an inner lining of brown wood, the slight, subtle fragrance of which proclaimed it cedar.

My wife and I straightened up simultaneously after the first disappointing glance and looked at Rothie.

'Why—it's empty,' said my wife.

He nodded his big head gravely, and then stood looking down into the empty box in so absorbed a fashion that I said to myself 'He expected to find something there and is puzzled as to what has become of it.'

'Something amissing, Doctor?' I asked.

'Nothing . . . I want to leave it with you for three or four days. Keep it open. Examine it. And, I beg of you, take every care of it.'

'Won't you explain the mystery?'

'Later. Perhaps you can fathom it for yourselves. It is better worth hatching than your china egg.'

And with that, and with that same strange softening of the rugged face which had found its way into his voice, he went.

'What a curious idea!' said my wife, looking down into the box when she returned from seeing him to the door. 'I can see nothing but an empty wooden box—cedar too. But there is nothing in that. It is perhaps thicker and more stoutly made than those one buys in the shops. I wonder—perhaps there's something underneath the wood.'

'If there is it's not meant to be tampered with,' for across the top of the cedar box were two bars of the same steel-blue metal chased with gold— one running exactly midways the length of the box, the other crossing it at right angles about three inches from the end. I had already tried them with a cautious finger and found them inviolable. By some deft craftsmanship they seemed an integral part of the outer case. The cedar box had certainly never been outside it since they were placed in position.

'Well, it's certainly a lovely old box,' was my wife's conclusion. 'But it's all very odd. What does Dr. Rothie expect it to do for you, I wonder?'

I thought I gauged his intention, but as a matter of fact I came nowhere near the meaning of it.

'Shall I close it up?' asked my wife, when she had packed me up for the night.

'Rothie said leave it open. We'd better

follow orders,' and the box was left standing open on the table by my bedside.

The days, black with gloomy thought, had been long ; the nights blacker and longer still, solid, interminable, uttermost depths of darkness. None but the sick and sleepless know how the shadows can ride the weary soul when the rest of the world is sleeping.

I had had many bitter bad hours in the nights, when the burden of life seemed too grievous to be borne,—when there was nothing to relieve one's thoughts for a moment from the useless weariness of their convict rounds,—when faith and hope burned dimmer than the night-light, and prayers availed not for their brightening,— when Death was the best of friends, and final rest the only thing left to long for.

But this night, strangely enough, I slept sound refreshing sleep, for the first time in many weeks.

The night-light glimmered on the dim gold chasing of the steel-blue box, and here and there tiny gold eyes winked back at it as though they were heliographing to one another. Then there would be intervals when they were probably uncoding and making up their answers, and then the wick would give a spurt and the messages flashed to and fro like lightning, and I lay and wondered dreamily what it was all about. The faint fragrance of the cedar came to me at times like a breath of Lebanon.

I was thinking of the box when I fell asleep. My waking eyes fell on it. Drowsily I thought I had dreamed of it. What, I could not recall, but the sense of it was vaguely pleasing.

'You've had a better night,' was my wife's greeting, as soon as she set eyes on me.

'Yes, old Rothie's charm is working, though I can't tell how.'

But I came to the conclusion that it was all quite simple.

Rothie had seen the need of some distraction for my thoughts and had provided it in the form of this curious old box. His quiet air of mystery was of course part and parcel of his scheme.

Very well, let it work, and I would help it all I could. To have had so restful a night was in itself mighty gain and worth pursuing.

Unconsciously I began to weave odd fancies round the damascened box; and from old custom, and so that the fancies might at all events have legs to stand on or wings to fly with, I got my wife to bring me the necessary volume of the encyclopædia and to read to me of Damascus and the ancient art of damascening.

Without a doubt old Rothie's charm was working.

So Damascus dated back to the days of Abraham ! And the art of damascening originated in Northern India and was established at Damascus in the reign of the Emperor Domitian, some time in the first century !

This ancient box might obviously then go back a very long way indeed. And the things it might have seen—if only it had been gifted that way !—Vespasian, Trajan, the Crusaders, Louis of France and Conrad of Germany, perhaps Richard of England, and Tamerlane who carried away the cleverest damasceners to Samarkand ; and later, many a tragic time 'twixt Moslem and Christian !

And was it not at Damascus, in the street called ' Straight,' that a certain Ananias went reluctantly to the house of Judas for the relief of one, Saul of Tarsus, a man of ill repute in those days, but held for better things ? And later, had not this same Saul, having forsaken the old things for the new, to be let down from the walls of this same Damascus by night in a basket in order to escape the too-pressing attentions of his former associates ?

Having got to St. Paul, my hand went naturally to the shelf above the head of my bed, and groped there till it found without any difficulty —so accustomed is it to that same search—my copy of Myers' most wonderful poem. And where I opened I read :

> *' What can we do, o'er whom the unbeholden*
> *Hangs in a night with which we cannot cope ? '*

That appealed. It hit me off to a nicety. If ever the unbeholden hung over any man in a night with which he could not cope, it surely did with me.

> *' What but look sunward, and with faces golden*
> *Speak to each other softly of a hope ? '*

The sun of my hopes had sunk behind the blackest of clouds. Now in the daylight, it was less impossible, if also less valorous than it had been in the night, to think of his possible rising again.

> ' *Can it be true, the Grace He is declaring ?*
> *Oh, let us trust Him, for His words are fair !*
> *Man, what is this, and why art thou despairing ?*
> *God shall forgive thee all but thy despair.*'

Yes, that got home too, for surely I had been most desperately despairing—an unforgivable sin ! ' This is my infirmity,' cried old Asaph the Singer, the leader of David's choir, and I felt myself akin to him. Maybe he was sick and thought he would never write another song for Jeduthun, the chief musician. And here was something more, and to the point :

> ' *Quick in a moment, infinite for ever,*
> *Send an arousal better than I pray ;*
> *Give me a grace upon the faint endeavour,*
> *Souls for my hire and Pentecost to-day !*'

Send an arousal better than I pray ! Just what I wanted, and wanted badly.

And as my fingers turned the well-known pages, I came on this also :

> ' *Eager and faint, empassionate and lonely,*
> *These in their hour shall prophesy again :*
> *This is His will who hath endured, and only*
> *Sendeth the promise where He sends the pain.*'

24

Great words, my masters—golden thoughts in jewelled words! They chased the darkness of my soul as those ancient craftsmen of Damascus chased that wonderful casket—wounding it first with sharpest chisellings, then salving the wounds with purest gold. They roused me from my hopelessness, and started trains of thought which were sweet to my heart as springs in a thirsty land.

It was the first profitable day I had spent since the ropes slackened. Profitable, that is, from my point of view. Who shall venture to deprive of their full and proper value the days we look upon as wasted?

And tracing back, I saw that it all came out of that strange old box of Rothie's, and I smiled quietly to myself at the shrewd old fellow's acumen.

That night again was a beneficent one. I slept soundly, and yet I knew when I woke that I had dreamed dreams and seen visions, for my brain was at work again, tentatively delving and sowing in its chosen field—and it seemed to me that it was a larger field than before, and that the delving went deeper and the seed was more choice.

For three clear days Rothie left me solely to the cure of the damascened box, and when he did at last favour us with a visit he showed less surprise at my surprising renascence than one might have expected.

As it happened, he caught me hard at work. For, some time in the early morning, the thoughts and fancies my mind had never ceased to weave around the silver box had crystallised into so definite a shape that, falling asleep still full of them, it had dreamed a dream.

And, what is more, when I awoke, the details of it were all so sharply etched upon my memory that I knew from old experience that there would be no peace of mind for me till it was all set down on paper. It is at such a time, when what has been vouchsafed to one insists on expressing itself, that the writer's joy is at its fullest.

So, at the earliest possible moment I had, for the first time in many weeks, called for pen and paper, and had rejoiced greatly at finding myself once more at work.

I had just finished writing when Rothie came in.

'That's all right. I don't need to ask if you're better,' he began, with a benignant smile.

' Yes, I'm fine ; but I've been dreaming about this, and I'll have a relapse unless you tell me all about it,' and I nodded towards the box.

He nodded understandingly. ' I know. And I'll tell you all I know myself —— '

' Is it magic of some kind ? ' asked my wife, in the wonder of my new lease of life. ' Where did you get it ? Have you found it act the same way in other cases ? Sit down and tell us all about it. It's Damascus, isn't it ? '

' Yes, Damascus of the first century.'

' Steel ? '

' No, silver. That wonderful depth is simply the result of age. The inlay is, of course, pure gold.'

' It is worth something, then.'

' It is perhaps the most precious purely material thing existent at this present moment,' he said very softly and deliberately. And she stared at him in surprise.

For a matter-of-fact, level-headed medico, his voice and manner as he said it, expressive beyond words of a conviction that admitted of no shadow of doubt, were strangely impressive. Then again, you must remember, he was a hard-headed Scot, not given to sentiment, still less to any

27

display of feeling, though we knew by long experience that the heart he hid so carefully beat more warmly than most.

'But,' he continued, 'this outer case, beautiful as it is as a mere work of art, is nothing. It is only the husk —— '

'But there is nothing else,' said my wife, looking up at him with a puzzled face, ' —except the cedar box.'

'Nothing else—except the cedar box.'

'Exactly !' said I. 'The cedar box.'

'Why, Jack, what do you know about it ?' asked my wife.

'I've just been trying to write the history of the cedar box as it came to me in the night.'

'Let us hear your version,' said Rothie, mightily interested. 'Then I'll give you the authorised.'

And I read them these notes of what I had seen in the night.

I was in an Eastern land. And it seemed to me that I was native there. I wore the dress of the country, spoke its speech, and was quite at home in all its ways.

I was sitting on a wooden seat in a carpenter's workshop. It was a simple workman-like place, but with a charm about it beyond the charms of any other carpenter's shop I had ever been in, and carpenters' shops and saw-mills have ever been dear to me. This was due no doubt in part to its situation. The upper portion of the wall, where the working-bench stood, was quite open. Whenever the worker at that bench lifted his eyes from his work they lighted on a view of uplifting and ever-changing beauty.

From that wide opening in the wall the narrow valley ran straight towards the setting sun. The bare, round summits of the hills on either side gleamed like silver. Here and there along their slopes I saw soft dark patches which I knew were Lebanon cedars. In the valley below the corn-fields glimmered like sheets of gold, the scattered houses were almost lost among their gardens and hedges of cactus, and their orchards of pomegranate and orange, and fig and olive ; and over them all the light of eventide was falling like a blessing, in a soft golden haze.

The workshop was ankle-deep in wide-flaked shavings of oak, chippings of ash, long creamy screw-spirals of pine, and the shorter brown-pink curls of cedar, and the sweet fresh fragrance of these was in the air. Outside were wheels, and yokes for oxen, in various stages of construction.

The sun was sinking towards the western ridge which closed in the valley. His beams came in through the opening above the work-bench in level golden shafts.

At the bench, in the full radiance of all that glory, a boy wrought all alone, so intent on his work that he barely looked up even when he spoke.

'It is for her, you see,' he said, with a quick smiling look at me,—evidently in reply to some remark of mine which the dream did not yield me.

He was a sturdy boy of twelve and very pleasant to look upon,—comely of face, and brown of skin through great friendship with the sun and air; brown-eyed, and every time his eyes glanced at me I found in each of them a radiant spark like a little golden star. It seemed as though a great glowing soul dwelt within him and shone out through those starry brown eyes. His hair, too, was brown and had a ripple in it.

He was dressed in a loose white garment,

30

girded at the waist with a carelessly-knotted cord, open at the neck, and coming down only to his knees. His legs and feet were as brown as the cedar shavings, and he wore the small roughly-tanned sandals of the country.

The work he was just finishing with such absorbing care was a small oblong box of cedar wood. As he turned it over and over in his hands, and ran his eyes and fingers along its sides and joints in search of slightest imperfection, I saw two things : First, that the box was very beautifully fashioned, without nail or peg,—sides and bottom all dovetailed into one another in a way that betokened considerable skill and long and patient labour. And, secondly, that the hands which had made it were very finely shaped, at once strong and delicate, and very gracious and gentle in their touch. The eager little fingers were soiled with work at the moment, and one of them, on the left hand, had a bit of rag tied round it. But in their handling of that cedar box they seemed to me instinct with loving sympathy as well as boyish pride of accomplishment.

A door opened off the workshop to an inner room. And through this door a sweet, low voice called, 'Leave thy work now, my son. The supper is ready and thy father and I await thee.'

'In one little moment, mother. I am just finishing,' cried the boy, and smoothed a tiny roughness on his box with a plane, and passed his fingers searchingly along it again, and ran his eye carefully over every inch of it to make sure.

'It is for her, you see,' he said to me again, with his starry glance and smile. 'And so it must be flawless.'

'To whom art thou speaking, my son?' came the voice through the door again. 'Who is out there with thee?'

''Tis a wayfarer,' said the boy. 'Perhaps he will eat with us,' and he smiled across at me once more.

And at that I heard them rise from their seats within, and they came to the door of the workshop.

The boy's mother was a woman of about thirty, I judged, very sweet of face and of a comely figure. She wore an outer robe of blue over an under-garment of rose, and on her head was a veil of white linen which fell down over her shoulders. Her eyes were brown like the boy's, but in them was a look which I could not at once fathom. There was in it an outreach, a farawayness, a touch of wonder, perhaps something of apprehension, as though she were subject to constant surprises and never quite sure what to expect.

The father was behind her. He but glanced over her shoulder and said a word and went back to his seat. I got no more than a glimpse of a bearded face and a pair of dark eyes.

'Where, then, is thy wayfarer?' asked the mother, looking round.

'Why,—on the bench there by the big saw,' said the boy, with a nod and a laughing look at me.

'But I see no one here,' said the boy's mother, gazing very earnestly at him.

'No?' he said in surprise, and smiled at me again. 'That is strange, now, for I both see him and speak to him, and he sees and hears me. I must have thought him, for he is very real to me.'

'Thou hast such strange thoughts at times, my son,' she said gently. 'Put away thy tools now. Thou hast wrought late to-night. Thy work will keep till to-morrow.'

But the boy suddenly fancied he had detected another tiny flaw in the side of his box, and bent over it with his plane again.

'And thou art always telling me—"The day's work in the day,"' he laughed merrily.

'Yea, but this could surely be to-morrow's work just as well as to-day's.'

'Nay, then, for when the sun sets it is thy birthday, and this is for thee. Now,'—with a final careful scrutiny with eye and finger, just as the sun dipped behind the western hills and the long narrow valley filled in an instant with plum-purple shadows, 'it is finished, and it is thy birthday,' and he joyfully placed the cedar box in her hands.

'For thee, mother,' he said again, with dancing eyes. 'And I made it all with my own hands—all for thee.'

'It is a marvellous box for one so young to make,' and she examined it with loving pride.

'My father taught me, you see, and it has taken me many weeks to make.'

'I thank thee, my little son, and I will keep it for thy sake as long as I live. It is the most beautiful box I have ever had. Surely there is not another like it in all the world.'

'I put my heart into it because it was for thee.'

'It lacks but one thing,' she said, as she slipped

34

the lid out of its groove and examined the box again, inside and out.

'What, then, mother? What lacks it?' he asked quickly. 'I thought I had ——'

'Thy name on it as its maker, little son. It is so marvellous a box that some might doubt ——'

'I will soon remedy that,' and he seized a slender gouge and a mallet.

'To-morrow, then. Come now and eat.'

'Nay, the sun is set, but I can finish it before the first star shows. 'Twill take me but a moment.'

He turned the lid upside down, and as he wrought on it with gouge and chisel—I awoke.

Rothie had listened with keenest attention. When I stopped he nodded his head gravely, and said :

'That is really very curious. You will hardly appreciate how extraordinary it is till you hear the actual facts. Listen! Some years ago I had as a patient an old man named Isaacson—Isaac ben Isaac, to be quite correct, but simply old Isaac Isaacson to the world at large. He was a Christian Jew and traced back without a flaw through generations of Isaac ben Isaacs right up to the very first Isaac, son of Abraham. His family tree, inscribed on parchment rolls, was monotonous enough to look at, but he was naturally very proud of it in a quiet way, and prouder still of the fact that the Isaac ben Isaac of the years 6–97 A.D. had risen above the material hopes of his race and had accepted Jesus of Nazareth as the promised Messiah.

'I won't go into details of his family history. As Christians its members suffered persecution and death, but always some survived to carry on the faith.

'My dear old patriarch completed his hundredth year and he was the last of his line. Wife, sons, and daughters, all had gone before him. He had other relatives, of course, but they were not in sympathy with him.

'I attended him for many years. There was never anything much wrong with him, but when one passes the allotted span by a generation it is perhaps well to have a doctor for a friend. And we had come to be on terms of the closest friendship.

'He was a most delightful old fellow. I never heard a complaint from his lips. He was at all times calm, quiet, dignified—at peace with God, with himself, and with all the world, even with his relatives who despised and hated him.

'And that Damascus casket stood always open on a table by his bedside.

'I had often admired it and spoken about it. Whenever I did so, he always wore a strangely uplifted look—a kind of exaltation of the spirit in some knowledge not possessed by others. I can hardly describe it, but his fine old face seemed to glow with some inner radiance, and his frail body to expand as though the spirit within grew almost too large for it. He was so good to look upon at such times that I used often to speak of the casket just in order to see him so.

'He died on his hundred and first birthday of simple old age, in full possession of all his faculties, and his passing was wonderfully sweet and beautiful.

'As I sat by his bedside, he looked at that casket with the look on his face that I knew so well, and he said " I am the last. You are to have that for the love you have borne me. It is a good thing to have. You will treasure it for its own sake——"

' " For yours chiefly," I said.

' " I am nothing," he said softly. " But that is much. I think it brings peace and a quiet mind. It has been very dear to me and to all my house for many generations . . . You will wait with me now. It cannot be long. And then you will take the casket with you, and a letter I have written about it. And when you have read the letter you will not fail to cherish the box. There are others . . . If it fell into their hands . . . It is not mentioned in my will, but my lawyers have drawn up a deed of gift which I have executed. Guard it very jealously, my friend . . ."

' I took the box home with me when he had gone, and the letter. This is the letter :

' The cedar wood box enclosed in the damascened silver casket I had from my father, Isaac ben Isaac, who had it from his father, who had it from his father, and so it has come down through all the generations of our house, from the days of Isaac ben Isaac who lived in Jerusalem in the time of Tiberius and died in Ephesus in the year 97. Which Isaac ben Isaac was the friend and disciple of John, the son of Zebedæus and Salome, who was sister

38

to Mary the mother of Jesus. It was to this John, His cousin and much-loved disciple, that the Master commended Mary with almost His last words, and John took her to his home and tended her as a son until her death.

' It was after her death and just before the persecution drove him to Patmos, that he gave to Isaac ben Isaac the little cedar box, and it was Isaac ben Isaac who enclosed it in the silver casket which he made, and wrought, and chased entirely with his own hands, he being a silversmith and no mean craftsman as the casket proves.

' But the silver casket, beautiful though it is, is nothing. It is but the body, of which the cedar box may be likened to the soul.

' For this little box was one of Mary's most cherished possessions, and she told John that it was made for her as a present by her little son, Jesus, with His own hands in His father's workshop at Nazareth.

' In confirmation of this you will find, in the lower right-hand corner of what appears to be the bottom but is in reality the lid placed thus for safety, inscribed evidently

with gouge and chisel, in Hebrew characters,
THE NAME :

יִשׁוּעַ

' And this is, as far as I know, the only piece
of the Master's writing in existence.

' We have treasured and reverenced this little
box through all our generations in remembrance
of Him.

' Do you the same ! For it hath in it a
virtue and a comfort beyond any words of man
to express.'

We sat gazing in silence at the little cedar
box, as Rothie carefully folded and put away his
letter ; and, for myself—no, I could not possibly
explain what I felt. I was stirred to the depths.

' How very strange and wonderful ! ' murmured my wife at last, in an awestricken whisper.

' You think it is beyond doubt, Doctor ? '
I asked, in a whisper also ; for that little wooden
box, in the light of this disclosure and my own
strange dream, was lifted above the realm of all
ordinary mundane matters and it lifted us with it.

' Quite. I accept it absolutely, as my dear
old friend did.'

'It is the most wonderful thing in the world then—a treasure beyond all price.'

'The most wonderful thing in the world,' he said softly, 'a treasure beyond all price.'

'Where do you dare to keep it, Doctor?' asked my wife. 'I should be almost afraid ——'

'When it is not in use I keep it in a Safe Deposit—and, after a hint I had from ben Isaac's solicitors, it is not in my own name.'

'May we see the—the Name?' asked my wife, in the same awed voice.

He took out one of those tiny pocket electric torches—the incongruity of it !—and illuminated the inside of the cedar box, and in the right-hand bottom corner we could with his assistance just make out the Name—the Name that is above every name—carved in the wood as a boy might carve it with gouge and chisel.

'Well, whether it is so or not,' I said, with no little emotion, 'I most certainly can testify that it hath in it a virtue and a comfort beyond any words of man to express. I have been a new man since you brought it into this room. Have you found it affect others in the same way?'

'I have. But you can understand that there are very few with whom I would care to leave it,

—only where I have reason to believe in the result.'

' I am very grateful to you, Doctor Truly it has done great things for me. I feel as if I could write as well as I ever have done.'

' Better, my boy, better ! ' he said heartily. ' What you have gone through will take you a great deal farther than if you had never been there.'

And, after allowing us a last long look at the cedar box, he reverently locked the casket and folded it with tender care in its various wrappings.

' I'm going up home for a day or two,' he said, as he tied the last knot.

' To Scotland ? ' said my wife, with a soft inflection of nostalgia in her voice.

' Ay !—to the Land of the Leal, as the young lady mistakenly called it, though indeed she spoke truer than she knew. For so it is.'

' And you are taking this with you ? '

' Not this time. It has made the journey many times, but for the special purpose for which I took it, it is no longer needed. . . . A very dear old aunt of mine realised her heart's desire yesterday. She was eighty-two and had been an invalid for over twenty years, suffering always and longing hopefully for the better things beyond. Now she has attained them and is completely happy. The cedar box has comforted her many times. Now she is with the Comforter Himself and no longer needs it. It will lie quietly in its secret place till I get back. . . . When I do,' —to me—' I'll look you up again, though you are out of my hands now. But take my advice and go slow for a bit. You'll go all the stronger and farther in the end. So I won't say good-bye but only au revoir ! '

We never saw him again. He was killed, as you may remember, in the dreadful fiery smash at Carnforth.

And the cedar box ?

Some day, perchance, when, after long waiting for overdue rent, and many futile applications to a name and address which have no longer any significance, a certain small safe in a certain great Safe Deposit is at last opened, and the contents disposed of in such manner as may be customary —the silver casket may pass into alien hands which will surely treasure it for its antique beauty, though ignorant of the Wonder of Wonders within.

And I have thought at times, when pondering this matter, that if it could only be discovered and left open in some sure and sacred place, that which emanates from it might do something perhaps towards counteracting some of the evil tendencies of the times.

But that, after all, is surely taking but a narrow view of the matter. For the Spirit knows no bonds or bounds, nor needs any assistance from material things. Silent and unseen, it is ever at work amongst us, and in time its leaven shall leaven the whole world and raise it to the heights of God's great hope and intention.

Printed in England at THE BALLANTYNE PRESS
SPOTTISWOODE, BALLANTYNE & CO. LTD.
Colchester, London & Eton

www.ingramcontent.com/pod-product-compliance
Lightning Source LLC
Chambersburg PA
CBHW020608260626
47157CB00003B/912